"I decided not to go away to college," Jeremy told his mom. "I'm going to stay in California to be close to you guys." *And Jessica*, he added silently, smiling to himself.

His mother let out a little, dry laugh. "Well, you might want to rethink your strategy," she said. She swiped a tendril of dark hair away from her face and looked Jeremy in the eye, her expression serious. Something about the look on her face made Jeremy's stomach turn violently.

"What is it, Mom?" he asked, now clutching the pencil. He felt his scalp tingle with anticipation as if there was some kind of danger in the air.

"Your father and I have come to a decision, Jeremy, and I'm not sure you're going to like it, but I hope you'll accept it." Mrs. Aames took a deep breath. Jeremy held his. "It's obvious your father's body can't handle the life we have here. The work, the money, the stress. It's all too much for him."

*Right*, Jeremy thought. *We know this. We've been over it a hundred times, and so far there's been no answer.* Then it hit him, and he froze up. His parents had come up with an answer, and apparently one he wasn't going to like.

"So, we're moving the family to Arizona," his mother said. She looked him directly in the eye to let him know exactly how serious she was. "And we're going to do it soon."

Don't miss any of the books in SWEET VALLEY HIGH SENIOR YEAR, an exciting series from Bantam Books!

*Visit the Official Sweet Valley Web Site on the Internet at:*

**www.sweetvalley.com**

# Francine Pascal's SVH senioryear

# Stay or Go

CREATED BY
FRANCINE PASCAL

BANTAM BOOKS
NEW YORK · TORONTO · LONDON · SYDNEY · AUCKLAND

# To Thomas John Pascal Wenk

RL: 6, AGES 012 AND UP

STAY OR GO
*A Bantam Book / July 2001*

*Sweet Valley High® is a registered trademark of Francine Pascal.
Conceived by Francine Pascal.
Cover photography by Michael Segal.*

*Copyright © 2001 by Francine Pascal.
Cover copyright © 2001 by 17th Street Productions,
an Alloy Online, Inc. company.*

*Produced by 17th Street Productions,
an Alloy Online, Inc. company.
33 West 17th Street
New York, NY 10011.*

ISBN: 0-553-49380-9

**Visit us on the Web! www.randomhouse.com/teens**

*Published simultaneously in the United States and Canada*

*Bantam Books is an imprint of Random House Children's Books, a
division of Random House, Inc. BANTAM BOOKS and the rooster
colophon are registered trademarks of Random House, Inc. Bantam Books,
1540 Broadway, New York, New York 10036.*

PRINTED IN THE UNITED STATES OF AMERICA

OPM     0 9 8 7 6 5 4 3 2 1

# Jeremy Aames

You know what I'm sick of hearing? Cheesy expressions like, "What doesn't kill you makes you stronger," "Bad things happen to the people that can handle them," or, "When life gives you lemons, make lemonade!" (Who's the dork that came up with *that* one?)

Okay, usually I'm a very positive person. I was positive when my father lost his job last year. I was positive when I had to work just to buy my family's groceries. I was positive when we had to shut down half our house because we couldn't afford to heat (or cool) the whole thing. I was even positive for my dad when he had his heart attack.

And eventually, things got better . . . for about five minutes.

Now Dad's back in the hospital, and I just don't understand what we're supposed to do. He stopped working so hard. He paid off all those overdue bills. He's been eating healthier. And he still has another problem with his heart.

If all that didn't make him better, what will?

# Conner McDermott

I had a problem with the whole twelve-step-program thing from the very beginning. I know I have to follow it to get better and all that. I know that. And I was perfectly ready to jump through whatever hoops the counselors at the clinic wanted me to jump through. I was.

Until I got to step two. "We came to believe that a power greater than ourselves could restore us to sanity."

After that, a lot of the steps have to do with God or this higher power and about accepting that it or he or she would help us through the trials of life and rehabilitation.

My problem was, I've always thought that people were pretty much responsible for their own actions. I want to drink, I drink. I want to drive fast, I drive fast. I want to break up with someone, I break up with someone. I never thought anyone but me was responsible for me. And it took me a while to get through all those steps.

But Alanna dealt with it. She was ready to ask some higher power for help and ready to ask him to "remove her shortcomings" (that's step seven). She was the one who helped me see what I needed to do. Not any overpaid, overfed, oversensitive counselor.

I don't know where I'd be without her right now. And I know they told us we really shouldn't date for a year after we left rehab. Something about making it on our own and the evils of codependency. But I really feel like I need Alanna. And if I can admit that I need someone, that has to be a good step.

At least that's how I see it.

# Alanna Feldman

I'm done with my twelve steps. Kind of. If I'm gonna be honest, I guess I have to admit I skimped on a couple of them. First of all, there's this one that's, like, totally unreasonable. It's number five: "We've admitted to God, to ourselves, and to another human being the exact nature of our wrongs." Okay, I had this whole session with my counselor, Chris? And I tried to admit the exact nature of all my wrongs, but it was hard. Because there are _so_ many. I mean, like, when I was drunk, I did a lot of things to a lot of people. How am I going to remember every single thing I did? And there are a few things I didn't want to talk about. Ever. So that was the first problem.

The second one is number ten. That's the infamous one where you're supposed to apologize to everyone you've ever wronged. I tried to do that. I did. But there's one apology I'm not going to be making anytime soon. And that's to my parents. I know there's some stuff I should apologize to them for. I'm serious enough about getting better to know that. But there's something that has to happen first.

First they have to apologize to me. For everything.

# Ken Matthews

It always starts the Monday before a game. It's like this buzz, this weird nervous excitement that starts in my heart, then moves on to a different part of my body every day. First my hands start to tingle, as if I can feel the ball in my fingers at all times. Then my legs are constantly jittery, like they're ready to take off at any second. Then, on the day of the game, it all goes to my head. I get this light-headed feeling, but I'm still so focused. Like I'm light-headed only because everything in me is focused on one thing.

Winning.

And going to school just makes the whole thing more intense. Especially when it's the championship that's coming up. Everywhere I go, there are painted signs cheering on the team. Some of them even have my name on them. It's so weird to walk into school and see a huge red-and-white sign screaming, "Go, Matthews!"

Weird and kinda cool.

How could I have ever thought of giving all of this up?

# Will Simmons

You know what I can't stand? This week. This whole freakin' week ahead of me. Everywhere I go, there are signs cheering the football team on to victory.

"Cage the Lions!"

"Go, Gladiators!"

"Go, Matthews!"

Please. Like he's the reason they're going to the championship game. Can we all just take a second and remember who the quarterback was that led the team to the first seven wins of the season? And does anyone realize that we wouldn't be anywhere near the championship game without those seven wins? Of course not. All they care about is their golden boy of the moment.

This time last year I was the hero.

I was the junior quarterback that brought El Carro High all the way to the championships where we <u>shut out</u> the Bears. Yeah, the defense dominated, but I was the one responsible for the thirty-eight points we scored.

"Each ball Will Simmons threw hit its mark like a receiver-seeking missile."

That was what they wrote about me. And now where am I? Nowhere. Not even on the bench. Things would be different if we were still at El Carro. We'd be the ones in the championship game, I guarantee that. But we're not there. We're at Sweet Valley High.

Sometimes I wish another earthquake would hit and take <u>this</u> place down.

# CHAPTER 1
Just Each Other

"Liz, check this out!" Jessica Wakefield said as she used her elbow to force open the slightly ajar door to her sister's bedroom. Predictably, Elizabeth was sitting alone on top of her light blue bedspread, her back propped up by a couple dozen pillows and her nose in a book. Whenever Elizabeth went through a little drama in her personal life, she could always be found reading, Like some classic literature was going to be the answer to getting over her alcoholic ex-boyfriend. Jessica couldn't even count the number of times she'd suggested a good night of dancing at the Riot and been brutally rebuffed. Sometimes the girl had no idea what was good for her. She didn't even look up until Jessica dumped her awkward armload of college catalogs on the foot of Elizabeth's bed.

"Check what out?" Elizabeth asked, lowering the tattered paperback just enough to peek over the top of the pages at her sister.

Jessica picked up the glossy SVU catalog and

flipped it open to a dog-eared page. She then presented the book to Elizabeth, who laid her copy of *The Unbearable Lightness of Being* aside. Elizabeth took the catalog and glanced down at the page in front of her.

"Cheerleaders," she said flatly. "You wanted me to see cheerleaders."

Jessica rolled her eyes. "No, look at the scholarships part," she said, flipping her blond hair behind her shoulder as she sat down next to her mountain of catalogs. "They give scholarships to cheerleaders! A lot of these schools do. How cool is that?"

"Yeah, cool," Elizabeth said. She handed the catalog back to Jessica and pushed a chunk of platinum blond hair behind her ear. "But do you really want to cheer in college?" she asked skeptically.

Jessica glanced at her sister. Was she serious? "Why would I *not* cheer in college?" she asked. She'd been a cheerleader practically since she could walk. She couldn't even imagine what it would be like going back to school in the fall without practices, without uniforms, without the roar of the crowd. It wouldn't even seem like fall without that stuff.

"I don't know. I've always thought of college as a fresh start, you know?" Elizabeth said, pulling the sleeves of her sweatshirt down to cover her hands, then tucking her hands under her arms. Jessica suddenly had the impression her sister was wearing a heather gray straitjacket. "No one knows you, so there's no preconceived notions of how you're going to act. You can be whatever you want to be in college."

Jessica arched an eyebrow at her sister and smirked. "Liz, is this your way of telling me that you're going to become a psycho biker chick next year?"

"No!" Elizabeth said with a laugh, her blue-green eyes losing a bit of their dullness.

"A nose-ring-wearing goth girl?" Jessica suggested.

"Yeah, right," Elizabeth countered.

"A raving slut?" Jessica shot back.

"Yes! You got me!" Elizabeth said, throwing up her hands. "That's exactly what I plan to be."

"Yeah, whatever," Jessica said, picking up the USC catalog. "Well, I plan to be a full-scholarship cheerleader with Jeremy Aames for a boyfriend." She smiled at the collegiate picture on the front of the catalog—four students standing in burgundy-and-gold T-shirts, looking all scholarly and obviously discussing something of major academic importance. Soon she and Jeremy would be two of those students. They'd be away from home, living in the dorms, doing whatever they wanted. No parents, no

HOJ. Just each other. She was so glad they'd decided to stay in California together. Life couldn't be more perfect. Maybe she'd even get eyeglass frames with fake lenses to put her in sophisticated-college-girl mode.

Jessica flipped open the catalog, inhaling the smell of the fresh, clean newsprint. "Some of these schools even have married dorms," she said as she watched the pages flip.

Elizabeth laughed. "Are you and Jeremy getting married now?" she asked. "Because I really think that as your maid of honor, I deserve some warning."

Jessica grinned and shook her head. "No!" she answered, happy to see her sister looking semialive. "I'm just saying if it ever *happened* to become an issue . . . we'd be covered."

She wasn't surprised when Elizabeth grabbed a pillow and whacked her over the head with it. "You're such a dork," Elizabeth said, picking up her book again. "But at least Mom and Dad'll be happy to see you're interested in your applications." She eyed the pile of books again, then looked up at Jessica. "So, where do you think you'll actually end up?" she asked.

Jessica shrugged, letting out a little contented sigh. "I don't know. I guess whatever the best school is that accepts both me and Jeremy," she said, looking her sister in the eye. "I'm just glad it's all settled. We're going to stay in California. We're going to be together."

*I can't believe I'm doing this,* Alanna Feldman told herself on Monday evening as she sank down onto the plush velvet couch in the TV room. *This is the low point of my life. Right here. Just don't let anyone walk in and catch me. Please. That's all I need.*

Having come to grips with the fact that she was about to do something totally horrible and shameful, she reached forward, picked up the DVD remote, and hit play. Images of a perfect spring day in a perfect southern town flickered onto the screen.

"But it's not quite so perfect, is it?" Alanna muttered, narrowing her heavily eyelinered eyes as the title, *Steel Magnolias,* scrolled onto the screen. She pulled the new Pottery Barn quilt her mother had purchased "on a whim" around her shoulders and clutched it under her chin. Watching this movie was a sadistic move, and she knew it, but she had to give herself a good excuse to cry. And that Sally Field funeral scene pretty much killed her every time. Not that she would ever admit that to anyone. But she *was not* going to cry over Conner. She'd risk getting caught bawling over a sappy movie before she'd risk *that.*

*I can't believe it's actually over*, she thought, grabbing an Oreo out of the half-empty bag in her lap and popping the whole thing into her mouth. It wasn't just over with Conner McDermott—it had virtually exploded. There were little bits and pieces of her heart and her hopes all over her front lawn. It was par for the course of her life, actually. Whenever she started to think someone might actually care about her, they either callously blew her off, went *Exorcist* all over her, or decided they'd rather move to New York with no money and no job than stay in California and deal with her.

Suddenly Alanna realized she'd stopped chewing. She was just staring at the pretty little rosebud patterns in the quilt as her eyes welled up with tears. She swallowed hard, the little dry cookie bits scratching her throat, then downed an entire glass of milk.

"All right, that's it," she said, wiping the back of her hand across her mouth to get rid of her milk mustache. She used the scrunchie around her wrist to pull her wildly curly hair back at the nape of her neck and stood up. The Oreo bag hit the floor, and a few cookies spilled out onto the new quilt, but she didn't care. She had to flee the pathetic aura of this room. She flicked off the TV and headed for her bedroom, determined to let either Hole or Nine Inch

Nails rip the sorrow right out of her through her eardrums.

But as she passed by her father's den, she stopped in her tracks. There, staring at her like a drug dealer determined to make a sale, was her dad's liquor cabinet. His *open* liquor cabinet. The little light that went on when you opened the door was shining at her like a tiny beacon—all the bottles in various states of fullness gleaming like brown and gold jewels.

*Unbelievable,* Alanna thought, bunching the hem of her long black sweater up in both hands. Not only hadn't her father gotten rid of all the alcohol in the house, the way her rehab counselor had instructed, he'd actually left the cabinet open. Alanna could have jimmied it open, as she'd done hundreds of times in the past, but that wasn't the point. Didn't he care about her getting better? Didn't he understand how *hard* this was for her?

"Of course not. He just thinks I'm a spoiled little brat who can't control myself," Alanna said aloud, walking into the den. "But you would think he'd at least want to protect his investment." He had, after all, paid a pretty penny to send her to one of the best clinics in the country. Only the best for his little girl. Actually, he'd only picked the place because if any of his rich friends ever *did* find out her dirty little secret, at least her parents would come off as heroes.

*Oh! But they sent her to such an esteemed place! They're such good, caring parents!*

Right.

"No one cares about me," Alanna muttered in a voice mixed with both sorrow for herself and disdain for the world. No one cared. Not her parents. Not Conner. Not anyone.

As she reached for a bottle of whiskey, a little voice inside her head started to speak calmly to her. *Don't do it. Call your sponsor. She'll talk you through it. If you do this, it's over.* She'd started to take a sip from the private supply stashed in her dresser last night, but then she'd immediately spit it out and gotten rid of the flask. Deep down, she'd still been hoping Conner would call and say he hadn't meant all the harsh stuff he'd said to her. But he hadn't called. They were through. There was no reason to hold back. *Except if you do this,* Alanna heard the voice continue, *then everything you've worked for is done.*

But at that moment she couldn't exactly remember why she'd done all that work in the first place. She grabbed the neck of the bottle, closing her fingers around the cool glass, and twisted off the top. She took a nice, long swallow, then another before the first one was even down.

Then she almost gagged.

Mouth and throat burning, Alanna quickly replaced the bottle and bolted upstairs, taking the steps two at a time. In seconds she found herself kneeling in front of the toilet bowl with her finger down her throat. After she'd cleared her stomach, she stood up and looked at herself in the mirror. Her eyes were watery and dazed, her nose was all puffy, and her cheeks were as white as the pristine bathroom tile.

"Pathetic," she said, sniffling loudly. She pulled a bottle of Scope out of the medicine cabinet and tried to fit the entire contents into her mouth. Then she glared into her red-rimmed eyes, waiting to see what she would feel. Disgust? Euphoria? Numbness?

And then an all-too-familiar emotion crept up her spine and settled in on her shoulders. All she felt was guilt.

Jeremy Aames leaned back on the hind legs of his chair and propped his feet up on his desk, expertly balancing himself in a kicked-back position. He'd been "studying" in his room for two hours and had so far managed to rack up a score of 162 in Nerf basketball, taught himself to twirl a quarter along the backs of his fingers without dropping it, and written the words *Notes for Shakespeare test* across the top of his notebook. The knock at his door came as a complete relief. He dropped the chair down, flipped open his book, and struck a studious pose before shouting, "Come in!" sounding exasperated, as if he'd just been interrupted in the middle of a brilliant thought.

"Hey, Mom," he said, looking up distractedly as she walked in. But the moment he saw his mother's drawn face, Jeremy dropped all pretenses. Something was up.

"Jeremy, we need to talk," she said, carefully perching on the edge of his bed.

Jeremy stiffened. *We need to talk*—four words you didn't want to hear from a girlfriend and four words you *really* didn't want to hear when your mother's just returned from the hospital where your dad is in the ICU.

"What's wrong?" Jeremy said, his pulse going from lazy to psychotically pounding. "Is it Dad?"

"No, no, no. Your father's fine, honey," she said wearily. Her lips flicked up at the ends for a second, then flattened out again. "I actually wanted to ask you about your application to the University of Arizona. I found it in the garbage."

"Oh," Jeremy said, leaning forward and placing his elbows on his knees. He fiddled with a pencil, passing it back and forth between his two hands. "Don't worry about that. I decided not to go away. I'm going to stay in California to be close to you guys."

*And Jessica,* he added silently, smiling to himself.

His mother let out a little, dry laugh, and Jeremy's brow wrinkled. His mother wasn't often wry. Or ever, actually.

"Well, you might want to rethink your strategy," she said. She swiped a tendril of dark hair away from her face and looked Jeremy in the eye, her expression serious. Something about the look on her face made Jeremy's stomach turn violently.

"What is it, Mom?" he asked, now clutching the pencil. He felt his scalp tingle with anticipation as if there was some kind of danger in the air.

"Your father and I have come to a decision, Jeremy, and I'm not sure you're going to like it, but I hope you'll accept it." She took a deep breath. Jeremy held his. "It's obvious your father's body can't handle the life we have here. The work, the money, the stress. It's all too much for him."

*Right,* Jeremy thought. *We know this. We've been over it a hundred times, and so far there's been no answer.* Then it hit him, and he froze up. His parents had come up with an answer, and apparently one he wasn't going to like.

"So, we're moving the family to Arizona," his mother said. She looked him directly in the eye to let him know exactly how serious she was. "And we're going to do it soon."

Jeremy's heart hit the floor and stayed there. He was sure it didn't beat for at least a full minute. "What do you mean, 'soon'?" he managed to blurt out.

"As soon as we iron out some details," his mother said. She stood and started picking up clothes from Jeremy's extra chair and folding them into a neat pile on his bed. Jeremy watched her, stunned, wondering how she could think about laundry at a moment like this. "Now, I know this is going to be tough on you kids, especially you. I remember how important senior year is, but I really don't know what else to do." She snapped a peach-colored polo shirt and folded it over her arm.

*How important senior year is?* Jeremy's mind was reeling. Did that mean she was planning on yanking him out of school before the year was even over?

"Mom, please, can you stop for a second?" he said, trying not to sound like a whiny brat. She placed the shirt down on the pile but didn't look at him. He stood up, trying to get her attention. "What does 'soon' mean?"

She sighed and hazarded a glance in his direction. "Within the next couple of weeks."

Jeremy's knees almost gave out, and for a moment he regretted leaving his chair, but he held his ground. "You have to be kidding me," he said, his brown eyes flashing. "What about school? And work? I can't just leave Ally like that. And what about basketball? Coach is gonna kill me—"

"Jeremy—"

"And what about Jessica, Mom?" Jeremy asked. His hands were starting to shake, so he tucked them under his arms. This couldn't be happening. He had to be dreaming. There was no way he was leaving Jessica. Not now. Not after everything they'd been through.

"I'm sorry," his mother said.

"So that's it?" Jeremy heard himself say. "I don't even get a vote in this?"

"I know it's not fair, Jeremy, but I'm scared," she replied. Jeremy noticed that she was wringing her hands. Actually wringing her hands, like they did in all the Shakespeare plays he'd been forced to read. Although all that work didn't matter now since he wouldn't even be around to take the test. "I'm scared for your father's life," his mother continued. "If we move to Tucson, we can help out my sister, Trina, with her restaurant. We won't be rich by any means, but the cost of living is lower there, and we'll be fine. And most important, your father will be fine."

"This isn't happening," Jeremy said, staring at the floor. "Can't we just wait a few months?"

"I'm sorry, honey," his mother said, reaching out and placing her hand on his cheek. Jeremy moved

13

his face away, and her arm dropped. She took a deep breath. "It really will all be for the best. You'll see."

Jeremy nodded blankly as his mother picked up a pile of dirty clothes and left the room, but his mind was fixated on one, piercing thought—

*Jessica's going to die. Or she's going to kill me. One or the other.*

# Will Simmons

<u>Things to bring to school tomorrow</u>
<u>to show Melissa:</u>

blue button-down

white button-down

gray tie

blue-striped tie

red tie

yellow-patterned tie

gray pants

tan pants


<u>Stuff to bring to work:</u>

notebook

pens (look prepared)

Power Bars


<u>Remember to:</u>

Repeat people's names when they
introduce themselves

Keep eye contact

Say "yes" instead of "yeah"

Not get bitter if Mr. Matthews starts talking about his perfect son

# CHAPTER 2
## Aames It Is

Will Simmons looked at his packed locker on Tuesday morning and wondered what he was thinking, bringing half the contents of his closet to school. Even if he did figure out what to wear to the *Tribune* this afternoon for his first day on the job, it would be wrinkled by the time he changed into it. School lockers were not made to comfortably store business attire. The hangers were dangling over the one hook, but he had to shove them in diagonally to even get the door closed.

"Hey, Will. Did you bring everything?" Melissa Fox asked, walking up to him with a familiar expression of efficiency on her face. She was holding up her chin and looking at him with the air of an executive about to critique his work. She'd even put her glossy brown hair up in a loose bun as if she was dressing for the part.

Will leaned over and gave her a quick kiss on the cheek. "Hey," he said.

"Hey," she returned with a quick smile. "So . . . did you bring everything?"

*So much for morning mushiness*, Will thought. But that was Melissa. He gestured at his locker, taking a step back so she could see. "What do you think?"

Melissa leaned over and glanced inside at the crammed clothing. She rolled her eyes and pulled out the two wire hangers that each held a shirt and a pair of pants. "You didn't bring the green shirt?" she asked, her brow wrinkling. "I love the green shirt."

"We're going to do this here?" Will asked, glancing around. He wasn't exactly comfortable with the idea of putting on a fashion show in the middle of the crowded prehomeroom hallway. People in this school already felt sorry for their pathetic, broken ex-football star. He didn't need the added humiliation of his girlfriend playing dress up with him in public.

"Where else do you want to do it?" Melissa asked, holding the light blue shirt up in front of her. "It's not like I'm going into the guys' bathroom."

So she had a point.

"This shirt, these pants, and this tie," she said, handing him back the blue shirt, yellow tie, and gray pants. Well, at least it was over quickly. How did she do that?

18

"Are you sure?" he asked, quickly stuffing his things back into his locker. "It's not too formal?"

"Will, this is the first day of your new career." Melissa smiled and leaned back against the lockers next to Will's, crossing her arms over the front of her formfitting blue T-shirt. "It's always better to be a little overdressed than underdressed. They'll think you respect them," she said. "If they're all wearing polos and khakis, you can wear that tomorrow."

Will nodded and pulled out the books he needed for the first half of the day. He was sweating a little bit along his brow line, and he was already feeling nervous about this afternoon. He just hoped he didn't screw up. He wasn't sure he could handle another huge disappointment.

At that moment, as if to punctuate his thoughts, a couple of freshmen from the boosters club walked over and hung a huge Go, Gladiators! banner on the wall directly across from his locker.

"Perfect," Will said, slamming his locker with a clang that made a couple of girls down the hall jump. "Just what I want to be looking at all week." He could feel all the blood rushing to his face just thinking about Ken Matthews taking the field on Friday in his place. If only he'd never gotten hurt . . .

Melissa pushed herself away from the wall and faced him, placing herself between Will and the offending poster. Good thing, considering he was already fantasizing about tearing it down and starting a bonfire with it in the middle of the gym floor.

"Look at me," Melissa said, squeezing his arm. Will obliged, looking down into her clear blue eyes. "Everything's going to be fine." She reached up and put her arms around his neck, flashing a reassuring smile. "You are going to do so great," she said in a soothing voice. "I'm already proud of you."

Will forced a smile and planted a quick kiss on her lips. He was glad, at least, that Melissa believed in him. That and this job were pretty much the only things he had going for him these days.

"Dude, did you see the way Jason Ryan went after that ball?" Trent Maynor asked, laughing as he pulled on his sweater after gym class. "I mean, it's *gym*, all right? Not the Olympics!"

"Yeah, I know," Jeremy said, only because he realized by Trent's tone that he was supposed to insert some kind of comment into the conversation. He stuffed his feet into his shoes as he tucked in his shirt. He wasn't sure what Trent was even talking about, but he also knew that when his best friend got on a roll, he became almost unaware of what was going on around him. Which at the moment was just fine with

Jeremy. The last thing he needed was for Trent to notice how morose he was and ask him what was wrong. Jeremy was not ready to talk about it.

"And *then* he gets up and does it again! The kid is still in the trainer's office, getting taped up!" Trent continued, checking his shaved head in the locker-room mirror. "That kid cracks me up."

"Yeah, I know," Jeremy said, then paused as he adjusted his shirt. Had he just repeated himself? The least he could do was vary his comments a little. But apparently it didn't matter because Trent was oblivious.

"And *then*—"

"Hey, guys!" someone stage-whispered, interrupting Trent's next gleeful rant. Jeremy's friend Stan was leaning around a row of lockers, and it was obvious from his wide-eyed expression that something interesting was going on. Usually in the locker room that meant someone was fighting. Jeremy sighed. He wasn't in the mood to watch a couple of guys pummel each other until the vice principal pulled them apart.

"Is it Roach and Peterson?" Trent asked, reading Jeremy's thoughts. "Those guys have been circling each other for days."

"No. It's not a fight," Stan said. "Anderson and Gilson are talking in the athletic office."

Trent raised his eyebrows. "They're coaches. It's what they do," he said dryly.

"They're talking about who's gonna be basketball captain," Stan said, leveling Trent with a look that said, "*Now* will you take me seriously?"

Trent caught Jeremy's eye and grinned. Jeremy just felt sick. It didn't matter to him who was going to be basketball captain. He was going to be gone before they ever even had a practice. But his friends didn't know that yet, so he grinned back and followed when Stan and Trent stealthily made their way to the athletic-office door. Jeremy briefly glanced at the exit as they passed it, wishing he could make his escape, but he'd have a hard time explaining it later.

His heart pounded with nervousness as they tiptoed up to the door. The last thing he needed was to get caught listening in on a private conversation and land detention. But when it came right down to it, the coaches were pretty dumb to be talking about this when they knew the locker room was full of guys. The only thing separating them from the athletic office was a thin wooden door with a huge, fogged-glass pane in the middle of it. Standing just to the sides of the glass, Jeremy and his friends could hear every word. They could even see the muddled shadows of Anderson and Gilson's porky frames.

"All right, so forget MacAffee." Coach Gilson's deep voice came through loud and clear.

"MacAffee?" Trent mouthed, scrunching up his face in indignation. Jeremy shook his head, attempting to tell him to keep quiet.

"That brings me back to Aames," Gilson continued. Jeremy's whole body went cold as Stan and Trent's faces lit up. "He's a good kid." Jeremy squeezed his eyes shut, unsure of what he was hoping for here.

"The best," Coach Anderson agreed. Stan snorted a laugh and slapped his hand over his mouth. "He was an excellent football captain. Even with all the personal stuff he went through at the beginning of the season, he stayed focused. I like the kid."

Trent and Stan were smiling and about to crack up. Jeremy felt himself start to blush from embarrassment, excitement, and total dread.

"Well, your recommendation seals it, then," Gilson said. "Aames it is." Stan and Trent jumped up and smacked into each other, a collision that sent Trent sprawling into the garbage can and made a noise that could have woken the dead.

Jeremy scrambled out of there so fast, he would have made both coaches proud. Once he, Trent, and Stan were safely back by their lockers and it was clear that the coaches hadn't followed them, Trent held out his hand for Jeremy to slap. Somehow he managed to do it.

"Do you realize what this *means?*" Trent said, so excited, he was oblivious to the fact that Jeremy was as white as his new gym socks.

"No one's ever been football captain *and* basketball captain in the same year, man," Stan said. He put his hands on his hips and pressed his lips together, regarding Jeremy like a proud father.

"Yeah, I know," Jeremy said, unsuccessfully attempting to swallow.

"You're gonna go down in history, J.," Trent said, clapping Jeremy on the back. "Dude, we're gonna have to celebrate!"

Jeremy nodded and forced a smile. All he could think about was how much he wished he'd never heard what he'd just heard. Because the only place he was going was Tucson, Arizona.


"I'm definitely going to school in New York," Tia Ramirez said after sucking a glob of pink yogurt off a plastic spoon. She stared off at the far end of the cafeteria as if she could envision the bright lights of the big city right there on the sea green wall. "I'd kill to live there."

*Shocker,* Conner McDermott thought, sighing audibly and shifting in his uncomfortable plastic chair. *We're talking about New York again.*

"Yeah, you were pretty much born to walk the

streets of the Big Apple," Andy agreed as he leaned back and laced his fingers behind his head.

Tia raised her eyebrows and leaned both elbows on the table. "You'd better not mean what I think you mean," she said in her favorite quasi-threatening tone.

"I mean in a strictly non-street-walker sense, of course," Andy said matter-of-factly. Tia balled up her unused napkin and tossed it at Andy's head. It bounced off and hit Conner on the arm. Conner picked it up and shoved it back toward their end of the table. He pulled his worn copy of *A Portrait of the Artist as a Young Man* from the pocket of his suede jacket and opened it up in front of him. If his two best friends were going to spend another lunch hour gabbing about their recent big weekend "back east," at least Conner could get some of his English homework done.

"Problem?" Tia asked him, addressing Conner for the first time since she'd asked him to pass the salt fifteen minutes ago. She eyed his book as if she'd never seen one before.

"No. Please. Continue your fascinating fifth-straight recap of your trip to the big city," Conner shot back, his green eyes flashing.

Tia grinned at him and flung one of her two thick brown ponytails behind her shoulder. "Great. I think I will!" she said. "Unless there's something you actually want to talk about—like maybe what's been up your butt for the past couple of days."

Conner knew this was Tia's way of expressing genuine concern for him, but he wasn't about to talk about what was going on between him and Alanna. First of all, Tia and Andy would never understand all the messed-up dynamics between him and his former almost girlfriend. And more important, they were also Elizabeth's best friends. All he needed to complicate things even more was for them to bring up Elizabeth. Nope. This, like most things, was something Conner should keep to himself.

"No, thanks," he said finally when he realized Tia was actually waiting for him to speak. He glared down at his book but continued to watch his friends out of the corner of his eye.

Tia and Andy both studied him for a second longer, then Andy scratched his red curly hair and shot her a what-are-we-gonna-do-with-him? glance. As if he didn't notice it. Tia shrugged, and they both turned their full attention back to each other. Conner felt his shoulders relax.

"So, have you heard from Rudy?" Andy asked Tia, returning to the modern art he was making out of his noodles and meatballs.

Rudy, no doubt, was yet another exciting New Yorker Tia and Andy had met on their trip.

"Not yet," Tia answered. She pulled her teal green cardigan off the chair behind her and draped it over her shoulders. "I hope he calls soon. I really want to hear how he's doing."

"Rudy is actually Rudolph Baker the Third," Andy said, leaning right and nudging Conner with his elbow. It wasn't as if Conner had asked, but he tried to appear interested—which entailed actually glancing up, for a split second, from the page he hadn't had a chance to read one word from yet. "He was this guy we were watching in the airport," Andy continued, undisturbed by Conner's lukewarm reaction.

"Yeah, we were playing that game where you pick a stranger and make up a whole name and history for him," Tia explained, her eyes sparkling. "He was all prepped out with a leather carry-on and a total Prince William haircut—"

"So we decided he was Lord Berkely of Andover Proper," Andy continued. "And that he was an heir to big British money, on his way to buy a movie studio in LA so he could finance a bunch of films about his mother's prizewinning family of Yorkshire terriers."

At this, Tia and Andy cracked up laughing so uncontrollably, Andy almost choked himself. Conner reached up and halfheartedly slapped Andy on the back.

"And this is funny because . . . ?" he prompted, hoping for a swift end to their utterly fascinating tale. Couldn't they tell he wanted to brood in silence?

"Because he ended up sitting next to us on the plane," Tia said, leaning forward and laying her heavily ringed hand flat on the table. "And it turns out he actually *was* rich, but he ditched his wealthy family, took the money he'd earned on his own while at school, and came out here to work for Habitat for Humanity. We thought he was totally spoiled just because of his cashmere sweater, but as it turned out, he couldn't *wait* to get away from his suffocating parents . . ."

" . . . and into a pair of cargo pants," Andy added with a smirk. "Can't judge a book by its cover," he said with a shrug. He glanced up at Tia. "But I still think he was gay."

Tia scoffed. "Please! He was totally checking out that blond stewardess."

"Come on!" Andy protested. "The guy totally wanted me!"

As his two friends continued to debate the sexuality of their new philanthropic pal, Conner felt a heavy, miserable guilt settle in around his heart. *Can't judge a book by its cover,* he heard Andy say again and again. That was exactly what people had always done to him—judged him because of his looks, his dress, his supposed attitude, or any other superficial thing—and he'd always resented it.

Yet that was exactly what he'd done to Alanna.

# melissa Fox

If I hear one more word about the championship game this weekend, I am going to tear out my hair. Of course, considering that I'm a cheerleader, I should be bald by Friday.

I just can't listen to it anymore. Everyone's all, "Ken this and Ken that." They're saying he's going to get that scholarship to the University of Michigan. The one that was supposed to belong to Will. They're saying he's a "hero of the gridiron." Ugh! Does anyone recall that he didn't even play in the first seven games of the year?

It should be Will getting all the credit and attention. He's the one who got injured playing for his team! He's the hero. What did Ken Matthews ever do?

Nothing. He spent the first few months of the year sobbing and being all pouty, and now he's the one on the all-state team while Will is going to spend his afternoons running around as Ken's father's lackey. It's not right. Ken and his father should be kissing Will's butt, not the other way around.

At least cheerleading will be over after this week and I won't have to act all perky anymore. It's hard to be perky when you're hairless.

# CHAPTER 3
## The Game Plan

"All right, guys, we're here to decide on a plan of attack for Friday," Ken said, addressing his teammates, who were seated in rows of black folding chairs in front of him. He pushed up the sleeves of his red-and-white SVH sweatshirt and hit the lights, dousing the locker room in hazy grayness. "If you see anything that you think will give us an edge against the Lions, speak up."

The guys just nodded solemnly as Ken popped the first tape into the VCR. Coach Riley had gotten them tapes of the Santa Carla Lions' last few games of the season, and Ken had suggested they all gather at lunch to get a head start on studying. Everyone had thought it was a perfect plan—figure out the game plan during the day, then start practicing it that afternoon. Ken had to fight to keep from smiling as he took a seat in the front row and hit the play button on the remote. At this moment he truly felt like a leader, and he definitely liked it.

"Okay, this is the game they won two weeks ago against Big Mesa," Ken explained as the game came to life in front of them. "Let's figure out what Big Mesa did wrong."

"And then try not to repeat it," Todd Wilkins said with a laugh. The guys all chuckled, then returned their attention to the game.

"Jeez, Santa Carla's defensive line stinks," Jim Cupples, one of SVH's defensive starters, said a few minutes later.

"Yeah! Check it out!" Todd agreed. He took the remote from Ken and paused the videotape, then pushed his lanky frame out of his chair and approached the television. "Santa Carla is great against the run, but they don't bring any pressure on the quarterback. Their front four are half the size of our offensive line." He pointed out the defensive linemen that were being totally dominated by the Big Mesa offense. Big Mesa's center was handling two of the guys on his own.

Ken leaned forward and narrowed his eyes as Todd unpaused the tape. He watched as Trent Maynor, Big Mesa's quarterback, completed a short pass down the sideline for a quick first down.

"So basically, we have to throw the ball as much as possible," Josh Radinsky said. He laced his fingers together behind his head and stretched out his long legs in front of him. "You ready to play, Matthews?" he said, a challenge in his voice. Josh was one of Will's best friends and showed almost no respect for Ken off the field. Ken didn't mind, though. As long as they worked together on the field, he could take any crap Josh wanted to ditch him on the side.

Ken smirked, never taking his eyes off the TV screen. "More than ready," he said. He continued to pay special attention to Trent, watching his every move. Trent called a play and dropped back to throw. He had all the time in the world. No one touched him, and he was able to easily find one of three receivers down the field. "Look at this," Ken said, gesturing at the screen. "Maynor could have killed them if he hadn't handed off the ball so many times."

"I guess that means I'll be getting some good rest on Friday night," Tony Lucia, the team's all-state running back, said with a grin. He crunched into an apple and chewed it loudly. "Maybe I'll bring some magazines to read from the sidelines."

Everyone laughed, but Ken stood up and flicked on the lights. "Sorry to burst your bubble, Tony, but I think you'll be getting some serious yardage in this game," he said.

Tony's brown eyes widened, and he was obviously intrigued. Whatever the guy joked about, Ken knew he loved nothing better than to pound away at defenders, break rushing records, and score as many points as possible.

"You know I got no problems with that," Tony said, placing his apple core aside and rubbing his hands together. "What did you have in mind?"

Ken could feel the adrenaline starting to rush through his veins as his teammates looked up at him expectantly. Part of him still couldn't believe he was even here. He couldn't even believe these guys were *listening* to him. It seemed like yesterday that the El Carro guys had all but tossed him off the field when they rallied behind Will, and Ken had felt like he'd never take another snap again. Now he was leading his team into the championship game. They were looking to him for the game plan. Unbelievable.

"Look at this," Ken said, pulling the *Tribune*'s sports section out of his backpack. He opened it up to the high-school sports page and held it out. There was a small piece about Santa Carla's senior lineman, Jake Barrow. He'd been injured most of the season but according to the article would be returning for the championship game. "This guy is close to three hundred pounds, but he's *fast*," Ken said, pointing at the picture of the huge Jake Barrow. "Coming off an injury, he may not have his best game, but they're definitely going to send him after me." He handed the paper to Josh, who whistled in awe when he got a better look at Barrow.

"Yeah," Ken said with a nod. He glanced at Tony. "We're gonna have to mix it up if we're going to beat these guys, so you'd better be ready to go."

Tony grinned and draped his arms over the two seats on either side of him. "I'm always ready, baby," he said cockily.

Ken and his friends grinned. "Let's put in the Palisades tape," Ken said. Todd killed the lights and Ken popped the new tape into the VCR, then rejoined his teammates in the chairs. At this point Ken could barely sit still. Thoughts of the game were taking over, and his whole body was tense with excitement. He was pumped—and he had a feeling he wasn't going to be able to sit still until he held that championship trophy in his hands on Friday night.

"So, who are you guys taking to the prom?" Drew Mitchell asked as he picked up a cafeteria chair, turned it around, and straddled it next to the table. Chris Robinson plopped into the seat next to him and dropped his backpack onto the table.

Jeremy and Trent glanced at each other, then looked across the table at Stan. "The prom?" Trent asked. "Is it May already?"

"Where have you guys been?" Stan asked, shaking

up his greenish yellow bottle of Powerade. "Everyone's been talking about it all day. Who's taking who, limos, hotels, parties—"

Jeremy slouched down in his seat and pushed his tray away from him. This was all he needed—talking about one more major event that he wasn't going to be around for. Did the world have it in for him or something?

"Ever since the theme was announced this morning, people have been talking dates," Drew said, grabbing a handful of fries off Jeremy's plate and shoving the whole wad into his mouth. "You've gotta plan ahead for these things."

"Start the weeding-out process," Chris concurred, clicking away at his electronic organizer. He held it out to Trent and Jeremy and pressed the little plastic pointer to the screen. "See, I've already made a list of the top-ten date possibilities. I figure, I start by taking one out a weekend, every weekend, until I know who the prime date will be."

Jeremy glanced at Chris, waiting for him to crack up laughing at his little joke. Chris just looked back at him, his blue eyes completely serious.

"You are sick, man," Jeremy said, eyeing his friend.

Trent laughed and grabbed the organizer from Chris's hand. "Nah, he's just practical," Trent said, scanning the list. "We don't all have guaranteed dates."

Jeremy's stomach churned. He couldn't take this anymore. He didn't want to think about the prom he wasn't going to. Or the amazing girl he wasn't going with. Or what it was going to be like to break the news to her.

"Guaranteed hot cheerleader dates," Drew clarified, not so stealthily snatching Jeremy's dessert.

Jeremy sighed and tried to clear the sudden image of Jessica in a sexy black prom dress, walking into her prom on the arm of some other guy, from his mind. Unfortunately the more he tried, the worse it got. He started imagining Jessica and the now perfect-looking scholar-athlete dancing under the romantic lighting, being elected prom king and queen, holding each other as they had their pictures taken, taking off for some wild after-prom party. He pressed the heels of his hands against his eyes and groaned.

"She got any friends?" Chris asked, raising his eyebrows, not noticing the torture Jeremy was putting himself through. Chris grabbed his organizer back and held the pointer at the ready as if Jeremy was about to recite a whole list of available SVH women's phone numbers and names by heart.

"You okay, man?" Trent asked, slapping him on the back.

"You know what? I'm not even going to be around for the prom, so maybe you can just take Jessica," Jeremy burst out, as if Trent's slap had hiccuped it out of him. It was a childish way to tell them, he knew, but he wasn't feeling very mature and grounded at the moment.

"Excuse me?" Trent said incredulously. "Where, exactly, do you think you're going to be on the ultimate cheesy night of our high-school careers?" There was a joking tone in Trent's voice, and Jeremy suddenly felt awful about the fact that Trent was about to be crushed. They'd been best friends since they were five, and Jeremy knew *he'd* freak if Trent was the one moving away. Trent was not going to be happy about this news.

"Arizona," Jeremy said, looking from Trent to each of his friends so they'd know he was definitely not kidding. "I'm moving there, like, next week."

The table fell silent, and Jeremy crumbled up a coarse napkin in his sweaty palm. He'd thought he'd feel better if he told them, but he just felt hollow as he stared down at the orange plastic tray in front of him.

"I can't believe this," Stan said finally. "Why?"

"It's a long story," Jeremy said, rubbing his forehead and then pushing both hands through his short black hair. "Basically my parents think my dad will be better off there."

More mournful silence. For the first time in Jeremy's recent memory, none of his friends were eating. Wow. He definitely meant a lot to them.

"You're not going anywhere," Trent said suddenly. His voice was so firm that Jeremy, for one second, believed him.

"No, I really am," Jeremy said, pushing himself up in his seat.

"No way, man," Trent said. "I have an idea. What if you come stay with me? You could have Ronde's room. He's not coming home at all next semester because he's doing that abroad thing in Australia. You know my parents love you. They'll definitely let you stay."

"Yeah!" Drew said, brightening. "It's perfect. You can just stay with Trent for a few months until graduation and then you can go to Arizona."

"There's no way your parents can say no," Trent said excitedly. "I mean, we'll beg. You know I have no shame."

"Well, that's true," Jeremy said, his mind racing. For a split second he got caught up in his friends' excitement. The Maynors were really cool people, and he'd spent so much time at their house over the years, they were practically a second family. This could really work!

But then his responsible inner voice kicked in

and Jeremy sighed. "I don't know, Trent," he said slowly. "I don't think I can do that to my parents. I mean, my dad needs us right now. I can't just ditch him."

The smile fell from Trent's face, but he obviously wasn't ready to give up. "Just let me ask them, J.," he said.

Jeremy shrugged and sat back in his seat again. He knew Trent would ask his parents no matter what he said, and he knew the Maynors would say yes. The problem was, it didn't really matter what the Maynors thought of Trent's plan. Jeremy had to stay with his family.

"You say *go* on the count of three! One, two, three, *go!*"

Jessica felt giddier than she had in her first season as an SVH cheerleader. She was in the middle of her best practice ever. She hadn't messed up once, and Coach Laufeld had even had her demonstrate one of her moves to the rest of the team because she was "the only one who had a clue what she was doing."

"You say *valley* on the count of three! One, two, three, *valley!*"

She was totally in sync with the rest of the squad, and she felt a crazy amount of adrenaline and excitement rushing through her veins. When the cheer was

41

over, she did her usual kick and yelled out, "Go, Sweet Valley!" Everyone on the squad turned to look at her like her head had just spun around. Usually those extraneous cheers were reserved for actual games, not practices on the baseball field. Jessica blushed and tucked her pom-poms behind her back.

"Sorry," she said sheepishly. "I'm just a little excited." She felt a strand of hair stuck to her forehead and pushed it away. She'd broken a sweat but wasn't even winded. Where was all this energy coming from?

"Well, you should be, Wakefield," Coach Laufeld said. "The rest of you should have half the energy Jessica does this afternoon. We're cheering in the championship game this weekend, girls. I want to hear you out there, got it?"

"Yes, Coach," the squad answered in unison. They sounded exhausted.

"Good," Laufeld said. She looked down at her clipboard. "Tomorrow we're going to try a new pyramid. Jessica, how would you feel about going up?"

Jessica grinned, her heart skipping a beat. She hadn't been at the top of one of their pyramids since the El Carro girls had infiltrated the squad. "Really?" she asked, glancing over at Melissa Fox and Cherie Reese, who were staring her down as always. "Absolutely," Jessica added innocently.

"Coach Laufeld," Melissa piped up. "I'm supposed to be the flyer."

She sounded more than a little bit whiny. Jessica glanced at Tia, and Tia rolled her eyes dramatically and rubbed her fists against her cheeks like a baby crying. Jessica put her hand over her mouth, hiding her smile.

"This is a team, Fox, not *The Melissa Hour*," Coach Laufeld said. Jessica had to bite her tongue to keep from laughing as all the color drained out of Melissa's face. Jade Wu didn't even bother and caught a silencing look from Laufeld for her giggles. "Besides, I haven't seen much energy from you lately," Laufeld continued, returning her attention to Melissa. "You might want to work on your attitude for Friday."

Melissa crossed her arms over her chest and shot daggers at Coach Laufeld. The coach just ignored it.

"Other than that, good practice, girls," Coach said. "I'll see you tomorrow."

As everyone gathered their things to go, Tia walked over to Jessica and slung her arm around her shoulders. "What are you on today?" Tia asked. "Have one too many Jolts at lunch?"

Jessica was bouncing up and down on the balls of her feet. "No. I'm just in a good mood," she said, leaning down to grab her duffel bag. "We're going to the championship game, Ken is starting, Jeremy and I are going to school together next year. . . . Life is good."

"Ahhh!" Tia said knowingly as they headed for the locker room. "It's the big J-man that's turned you into ultimate cheerleader girl."

Jessica smiled, swinging her pom-poms back and forth at her sides. "I can't wait to get to HOJ," she said, her heart fluttering. "I did all this research on colleges this weekend, and I can't wait to tell him about it."

Tia pushed Jessica away with a laugh and held up her hands. "Okay, you are just a total loser," she said. "I don't think I should get too close to you or you might rub off."

"What can I say?" Jessica said giddily, resisting the urge to twirl around like a schoolgirl. She did have *some* dignity. "Life is good."

# Andy Marsden

## The Cheerleader in All of Us

Ladies and gentlemen of Sweet Valley High, it's about time we all get something off our chests. Something we're all aware of but in many cases are afraid to admit. There is no reason to be ashamed of it, my friends. So let's just say it together, in one grand voice, like angels singing out together.

We all want to be cheerleaders!

I'm not talking about the pleated skirts, the flippy ponytails, or the inexplicable ability to be thrown into the air, keep a smile on the entire time, and trust a bunch of chicks to catch you as you come hurtling back to earth. No. I'm talking about the basic, primal urge to cheer for our team, to voice our support, to lend our lungs to the cause.

It's the natural response to championship week, my fellow Gladiators. You are constantly bombarded by spirit signs, football players wearing jerseys, sweats, and varsity jackets, actual cheerleaders overflowing with spunk. It gets inside us. It takes over. It makes us want to scream, "Maim the Lions!" at the top of our voices in the middle of history class. And you know what I say? Do it! Give in to the cheerleader within. Let his or her voice be heard. If you want to yell, "Go, Gladiators!" on the cafeteria line, let 'er rip. If you have the sudden urge to cartwheel down the hallway between classes, you have my blessing. Because it's all about football, baby. You know it. I know it. The cheerleader in your heart knows it.

Now it's time to tell the world. Sweet Valley High is going to kick some major Santa Carla butt this weekend, and as long as you give in to the spirit, you and your inner cheerleader will be partially responsible for the glory. So get out to the game this weekend and be a true Gladiator.

We'll even give the first five hundred fans a free pom-pom.

# CHAPTER
## I'm the Meat
# 4

*Okay, calm down,* Ken told himself as he crouched behind his center, Brian Cogley, on the field at practice. *Just call the play. Everything's fine.*

But as he lined up and looked down the line of offensive players at Coach Riley, he knew everything was not fine. Riley was pacing the sidelines like a caged tiger salivating for meat. And Ken was the meat. So far Ken had managed to fumble the ball once and get sacked twice—and practice had started only ten minutes ago. What had happened to that adrenaline he'd felt coursing through his veins earlier this afternoon? Was it really just too much caffeine? Maybe he didn't have a championship game in him right now.

"Just focus," Ken said under his breath. He called the play. "Blue thirty-two! Blue thirty-two! Hike!" Brian snapped the ball, and Ken dropped back to pass. All his receivers were covered downfield. *Damn, the defense is playing well today,* Ken thought as he bounced up and down, clutching the ball, looking for one play—any play. Apparently his video session had pumped everybody else up and made him into a fumbling idiot. Finally he saw Josh waving his arms and let the ball fly. Even as it was coming out of his fingers, Ken knew it was no good. He was too tense. He overthrew Josh by at least ten yards. Josh made a valiant play, diving for the ball, but he wasn't even close. He got up, dusted the dirt off the front of his practice jersey, and shook his head at Ken, disappointed. For once Ken had to agree with the guy.

"Matthews!" Coach bellowed. Ken squeezed his eyes shut and dropped his head back. *Here it comes.* "Get your sorry butt over here, Matthews!"

When Ken looked around again, he saw that every single one of his teammates was either staring him down as if he'd betrayed them or avoiding eye contact altogether. Ken was filled with a sick sense of shame and sorrow. Suddenly he wished he was anywhere but here. He flicked open his chin guard and let it dangle, then trudged over to the sidelines.

"Sorry, Coach," he said when he got there. Riley got right in his face—so close that the bill of his baseball cap knocked into Ken's helmet and the hat flew off the back of his head.

"Sorry's a good word for what you're doing out

48

there, Matthews!" Coach sputtered, his face matching the color of his crimson Sweet Valley windbreaker. Little tufts of hair were sticking up all over his head. "And sorry's too soft a word for what you're gonna be if I have to call you over here again, you got that?"

"Yes, Coach," Ken said quietly, eyes downcast.

"Speak up and look at me when you've got something to say," Riley yelled in full-on drill-sergeant mode.

"Yes, Coach!" Ken shouted back, managing to stare the man directly in his fierce eyes.

"I want to see some championship football out there!" Riley bellowed. "Don't make me sorry I let you back on this team." Ken felt like Riley had just taken a knife to his heart, but he tried not to react. Then Coach blew his shrill whistle right in Ken's face. "Okay, ladies!" he yelled to the guys on the field. "Ken's mind is not on his game today, so we're all gonna do twenty laps right now to give him some time to think!"

The team groaned in unison, and Ken was the unhappy recipient of even more threatening glares. As the guys grouped up and jogged over to the track that circled the field, Ken started off to join them, thinking it might be a good idea to lag behind a bit so no one would try to flatten him during the run.

"Where are you going?" Coach asked, grabbing his arm, his rough fingers digging into Ken's skin.

"You said to do laps," Ken answered.

"Not you." Riley shook his head. He pointed to the bench on the sideline. "You're supposed to sit and think."

Ken's mouth dropped open, and for a moment he didn't move, trying to figure out if Riley was joking. He had to sit out his own punishment laps? The guys would kill him for that.

"You're wasting precious time, Matthews," Riley said. Then he stood there and watched Ken as he walked over to the slatted bench and sat down hard. The team jogged by moments later, and Ken couldn't even look at them.

He pulled off his helmet and hung his sweaty head, trying to review plays and envision himself pulling them off. But he couldn't do it. He was doubting himself, and he couldn't stop the evil thoughts from seeping in. What if Coach was right? What if he shouldn't even be on this team? What if he let everyone down?

Mr. Matthews put his hand over the phone and glanced apologetically at Will. "Sorry about this, Simmons. I'll be off in a second," he whispered.

"No problem," Will mouthed back. He leaned

back in the cushiony chair across from Mr. Matthews's desk and sighed, letting the last bit of nervousness wash itself away with his breath. When he'd first arrived at the *Tribune* that afternoon, he'd been ready to come out of his skin from all the tension that had built up inside him all day. But Mr. Matthews had been beyond cool since the moment he'd met him, and Will was starting to feel at home among all the ringing phones and crazed people running around. He'd been so worried about his clothes, but everyone was so busy, they didn't even seem to notice he was there, let alone what he was wearing.

"Sorry about that, Will," Mr. Matthews said again, hanging up the phone. He put his hands on his hips and looked down at his disheveled desk but didn't sit down. It seemed like the guy was always on his feet. "What were we talking about?"

"How Wisconsin is going all the way next year," Will said, clearing his throat and sitting up straight.

"Yes!" Mr. Matthews said, punctuating with a thrust of his hand. "Thank you! How could anyone miss the fact that Wisconsin is primed? Ken thinks Michigan is going to take the title."

Will's forehead wrinkled in exaggerated surprise. "Michigan? They're good, but they don't have the defense." Of course, they did have an amazing offensive line that would make any quarterback look good. Which was why Will had been dying to play there . . . back when he could play. But that was all in the past. This job, this office was his future. He had to focus on that.

Mr. Matthews laughed and shook his head. "Would you please talk to my son?" he joked. Then he sighed and finally lowered himself into his chair, which let out a sharp creak. "But he's got his heart set on Michigan."

Will felt his face start to burn, and he shifted in his seat. "Ken's going to Michigan?" he asked, trying his best to sound like the answer wasn't going to kill him. Here it came. The my-son-is-a-perfect-player-with-a-perfect-future-and-I'm-a-proud-father speech.

"Hopefully," Mr. Matthews said. He was staring at a random point on his desk as if a few thoughts were flying through his mind at the same time. Will held his breath and waited for the painful jealousy to pass. He envisioned Ken running out onto the football field in a blue-and-gold uniform, the crowd going crazy as he took charge of the field. He was just about to see Ken run into the arms of a beautiful, scantily clad cheerleader when Mr. Matthews finally snapped out of it.

"Know what I'm gonna do?" he said, shuffling a

few papers and pulling out a sheet with long lines of tiny print all over it. Will tried to bring his mind back to reality. "I'm going to give you an assignment," Mr. Matthews said. He jotted down a few notes on a pad, then ripped off the top page and handed it to Will. "Normally you'd be doing nothing but filing for at least a month, but I like your style, Simmons. Always have."

"Thanks," Will said, coloring now with pride and embarrassment rather than jealousy. Until recently the two of them had never had any contact aside from a few reporter-player encounters, mostly last year when Will was at El Carro High. So obviously Mr. Matthews was talking about Will's style as a football player. It was nice to know that someone remembered his talent on the field. He was starting to forget about it himself.

Will looked down at his assignment. He was supposed to cover a girls' volleyball game in Palisades. Okay, so it wasn't like he'd been asked to cover college football or something, but it was a start. Who cared? He'd never expected to get a writing assignment this early on. Now if only he knew anything at all about girls' volleyball.

"If it's okay with you, I'm gonna go grab some issues and read up on how you guys normally cover these games," Will said, standing.

"Okay with me?" Mr. Matthews said, raising his eyebrows. "That's just the kind of initiative I like to see, Simmons."

Will grinned. "Let me know if you need anything," he said.

Then he strode out of the office, trying to remember from the quick tour he'd been given earlier where the huge room was that housed all the back issues of the paper. As he navigated the narrow halls of the news offices, Will's chest was suddenly filled with something he hadn't felt in a long time. Hope and pride. He felt like he belonged here, and watching Mr. Matthews in action had been so cool. For the first time since he'd been injured, Will felt inspired by somebody.

It was just odd that the inspiration happened to be Ken Matthews's father.


Jessica bounced up to the door to House of Java and held it open for a couple of scraggly skater guys coming up behind her. They flashed her looks of complete disdain as they passed by.

"You're welcome!" Jessica trilled with a hint of sarcasm. She walked in, tossed her bag on the floor behind the counter, and looped her arms around Jeremy's neck just as he turned around to greet her.

"Hey, Jess," Jeremy said, hugging her back tightly.

"Hey, yourself," she returned, inhaling the sweet smell of his T-shirt. One of these days she was going to have to find out what kind of fabric softener he used so she could buy some and keep a sheet under her pillow. "I have so much to tell you," she said, spinning and grabbing her bag full of college catalogs from the floor.

"I have something to tell you too," Jeremy said.

His tone made Jessica freeze. She turned around slowly and took her first good look at Jeremy's face. He was a little pale, and his eyes were looking into hers steadily. He was trying to prepare her for something. Something bad.

"Is it your father?" Jessica asked, the sound of her heartbeat filling her ears.

"No, not really," Jeremy said. "My dad's okay. . . ." He looked around the almost empty coffee shop. Daniel was over in the far corner, wiping down tables. "Hey, D.! Can you hold down the fort for a minute?" Jeremy called.

Daniel used his rag to salute, and Jeremy took Jessica's hand and led her into the back room. By now she was almost bursting with dreadful anticipation. What was so bad that they had to go into the back room to talk about it?

"You'd better sit," Jeremy said, walking over to the frayed, lumpy couch and sitting on the far end.

Jessica lowered herself numbly onto the other end of the couch, still clutching her bag in front of her. He was going to break up with her. That had to be it. She couldn't think *why* he was going to break up with her, but what else could this possibly be?

"What is it?" Jessica said, wishing he would just get it over with already. She felt suddenly exhausted, as if expending all of that crazy energy at cheerleading practice was finally catching up with her.

"I don't know how to say this, so I'm just going to say it." Jeremy wiped both his palms on the thighs of his jeans. He looked her directly in the eye, but she could tell it was taking him a lot of effort to do it. "My family is moving to Arizona. Soon. Sometime within the next couple of weeks."

All the air rushed out of Jessica's lungs. "What?" she asked, her eyes filling with tears. If there was one thing she would have never thought he was about to tell her, it was this. Moving? Wasn't this just a little bit out of nowhere?

"I know," Jeremy said. "I know this screws up all our plans."

Jessica looked down at the backpack in her lap and placed it on the floor next to her. Unfortunately, doing that left her feeling totally exposed. "Why?" she managed to say without any tears spilling over. "Why there? Why . . . why now?"

Jeremy sighed. He reached out and wrapped his fingers over the top of her hand. "My parents think my dad will be healthier there," he said. "That's the short version. My mom's convinced it's the only way to keep him . . ."

*Alive,* Jessica thought, a chill running down her arm. Neither one of them wanted to finish the sentence out loud, but they both knew what he meant. *This can't be happening,* Jessica thought, looking down at his hand covering hers. *He can't really be leaving.*

"I'm really sorry, Jess," he said, squeezing her hand and looking at her face with an almost hopeful gaze. Jessica wasn't sure exactly what he was hoping for, but at that moment she couldn't imagine ever feeling hopeful about anything again.

About a million conflicting thoughts ran through her mind. She wanted to cry, yell, and scream, but she knew none of those things would help the situation, and they would just upset Jeremy more. This was going to be awful for her, but she knew it was going to be ten times more crushing for Jeremy. He had to leave not only her, but his friends, his home, his school. When she thought about how awful that would be for him, she figured she could wait until she got home to cry and yell and scream.

She reached out and put her arms around him,

sliding over on the couch so she could hold him tighter. Jeremy buried his face in her hair and sighed.

"Don't say you're sorry," Jessica said, reaching up to wipe a tear from her cheek. "This isn't your fault."

"I'm gonna miss you so much," Jeremy said.

His voice cracked, and Jessica's heart cracked along with it. She knew she had to be supportive for Jeremy, but inside she felt like she was shriveling up. She was already nostalgic for ten minutes ago when she'd been the happiest person in California. Now all of her hopes and dreams for next year had been squelched in an instant.

Funny how she could go from happiest to most miserable in about sixty seconds.

# Jeremy Aames

I can say with no doubt whatsoever that telling Jessica about the move was the hardest thing I've ever done in my life. I get this hot, biley, sick feeling in the pit of my stomach when I just <u>think</u> about the look on her face.

And to know that I put it there . . .

I was debating all afternoon about whether or not I should let Jessica know about Trent's offer. I hate that I wasn't completely up front with her, but what would have been the point? If I told her I could probably stay with Trent, that would just get her hopes up. And there's no point in doing that. Because my family needs me. Okay, I know it's just for a few months, but what would Emma and Trisha do without me? And I'm sure my parents are going to need my help getting settled and everything. Staying in Big Mesa is just not an option.

Is it?

# CHAPTER 5

## An Un-Alanna Move

Alanna took the long route home from school Tuesday afternoon, delaying the inevitable as long as possible. The first three hours at home every day were the worst. There was nothing to do except listen to CDs and stare at her books. Of course, what came after that wasn't much better—a tense dinner with her parents, followed by either a lecture or worse—the silent treatment. Maybe her parents were right. Maybe she should become a joiner and sign up for a million clubs. At least she wouldn't have to come right home every day.

Back in the day—back before she got sober—Alanna almost never came directly home from school. She and her friends would spend their time trolling the mall, doing the occasional shoplifting, freaking out house moms by loudly talking about their parties and their exploits. Then they would usually end up at the beach or in someone's garage or basement or driveway, drinking and smoking and ensuring groundings and hangovers for themselves. Alanna felt herself tense up as she drove past one of her former boyfriends' houses. That part of her life was over. If she ever went back, she'd go back to everything that life entailed.

Alanna turned the car into her long driveway and slammed on the brakes in surprise. She was pulling up behind Conner's black Mustang. And Conner himself was lounging on the back bumper, his arms crossed over his heather gray T-shirt, his legs crossed at the ankle. He had this air about him as if he belonged there. As if it wasn't completely out of the ordinary to find a ripped-jeans-and-lug-boots-wearing guitar junkie just hanging out in the driveway of a ten-bedroom mansion. Damn, Alanna loved that.

With shaking hands, she managed to put the car into park. She tried to be nonchalant as she climbed out of the car, but her racing pulse seemed to have taken control of her limbs, making every movement jerky and awkward. Finally she just tucked her hands into the pockets of her tattered leather jacket to keep them from moving.

"Hey," Conner said quietly, pushing himself away from the car as she approached.

"Hey," Alanna said. They held eye contact for about half a second, and then Conner looked off over her shoulder and Alanna glanced down at her shoes, suddenly wishing she'd bothered to check herself out in the mirror this morning. "How long have you been here?" she asked.

Conner shoved his hands in his back pockets and shrugged. "Awhile."

"Oh," Alanna said, nodding. Well, this was a conversation to end all conversations.

"Listen," Conner said finally. "I'm sorry, okay? For everything."

Alanna's heart jumped, and she gazed up into his cloudy green eyes. "Yeah, well, you should be," she said, hedging. There was no reason to give in easily, even though her whole body was begging her to just crawl into his arms. "What do you mean, 'everything'?"

"Everything I said the other day," Conner explained, staring at the ground as he kicked at the asphalt driveway. "I was totally out of line." He looked up at her through his long bangs. "Forgive me?"

Alanna almost melted into a frizzy-haired puddle at his feet, but instead she just threw her arms around his neck. It was a completely un-Alanna move, but she didn't care. She'd never felt more relieved in her life. Conner was so surprised, it took him a second before he pulled his hands out from behind him and wrapped his arms around her. But when he did, he gripped her tightly. Alanna held her breath for a long time, not wanting to let this moment end.

But when he let go, it was okay. He was still there, and she could tell from his face that he wasn't going anywhere—at least not anytime soon. As they walked into the house together, a nagging voice inside Alanna's head told her to tell Conner about the drink she'd almost taken Sunday night, and more importantly the one she *had* taken last night. She needed to tell someone. And Conner deserved to have the whole truth. But with one quick shake of her head, Alanna talked herself out of it. It was so insignificant. She'd hated it. And she'd gotten it out of her system before it even had a chance to hit her stomach, so technically she hadn't really consumed anything.

She slipped her hand into Conner's, and he gave it a quick squeeze. So what if she'd felt that whiskey on her tongue all day today? Now that she had Conner back, she wouldn't need to drink ever again.

Ken slammed the door of his beat-up Trooper extra hard, then winced at the tinny sound it made in protest. One of these days his temper was going to cause that thing to fall right off its rusty hinges. He took a deep breath and slung his backpack over his shoulder, trudging up to the house. Practice had been torture, plain and simple. His body ached all over, not just from the strain he'd put it through, but from the added stress of feeling like everyone he knew was disappointed in him. All Ken wanted to do right now was grab some leftover Chinese out of the fridge, retreat to his room, and watch whatever crap they were showing on Comedy Central.

"Hey, Ken, how was your day?" Ken's father's voice boomed from the direction of the kitchen the moment Ken walked through the door.

Ken stopped in his tracks and for a split second wondered if he'd wandered into someone else's house. He looked around. Shag rug circa 1979? Check. Case of old and dusty football trophies? Check. Vague, sour, thus far unpinpointed smell? Check. Nope. He was in the right place.

"Hey, Dad," Ken said, walking tentatively toward the kitchen. He leaned against the doorjamb and watched as his father grabbed pieces of extra-crispy chicken out of a big red-and-white-striped bucket and laid them out on plates. "What are you doing home?" Ken asked.

"Believe it or not, I did everything I needed to do today, and I thought I'd come home and have dinner with my son," Mr. Matthews said, continuing to putter around with plastic foam bowls of potatoes and macaroni and cheese. Ken's stomach grumbled as his father finished laying out the meal and sat down at the Formica table. He looked up at Ken. "Gonna join me?" he asked.

Ken shrugged and placed his bag on the floor, both actions causing his muscles to twinge with exhaustion. He flopped into a chair and dug in. Within five minutes he was feeling much better. It was amazing the effect food had on his tired body. All he needed was a chocolate ice cream chaser and this day might turn right around.

"Thanks, Dad," he said, feeling suddenly grateful that this was the one day his father had decided to get domestic. He really needed some TLC in the form of KFC right now.

"You're welcome," his father said, smiling as he chomped on a chicken wing. "What a day," he said. "You know, the Simmons kid started at the *Tribune* this afternoon."

Ken paused with a forkful of mashed potatoes hovering inches from his mouth. Had he just heard right? Because the last person on earth he wanted to talk about right now was Will Simmons. "Yeah?" he said, hoping that was all his father had to say on the subject.

"What a good kid," his father continued, leaning back in his seat. "He's smart, he's driven, and I don't think I've ever seen so much energy from a teenager in my life." He sucked at his upper teeth once and glanced over at Ken. "You could take some tips from him, Ken," he said. "I'd like to see you have as much fire in your gut as Simmons seems to have."

Ken definitely had something in his gut, but it felt more like a big, fat rock than a fire. It took a few moments for him to swallow what was in his mouth, then he pushed away his plate. He was at a total loss for words, but luckily his father didn't seem to expect him to answer—he just went on gabbing about Will—his professionalism, his attitude, his *grooming*.

Silently Ken seethed, staring at his half-eaten food. For the first few weeks of the year he'd listened to his father rave about Will and his abilities on the field. All his dad had cared about was the fact that Ken should be the one out there leading the Gladiators to victory. He'd hammered it home over and over and over again—how disappointed he was that Ken wasn't playing, how Will seemed to have it all together.

And now. Now that Ken was doing everything his father had wanted. Now that he was the one taking Sweet Valley to the championships and getting written up in the paper. Now that people were coming up to Ken's father in the supermarket, telling him how much they admired his son. Now Ken had to hear about Will's abilities in the *office?*

"You should have seen the way he took on his first assignment . . . ," Ken's dad was saying. "He didn't even have to ask me what to do. It was just instinctive. . . ."

Ken shoved his chair back from the table noisily and got up, then crossed the room in three long strides.

"Where are you going?" his father called after him.

"I'm not hungry," Ken said, grabbing his bag and bounding up the stairs. He slammed his bedroom door behind him—this one making a much more impressive sound than the car's had. But it did nothing to calm Ken's sizzling nerves. He threw himself down on his bed and squeezed his eyes shut, but he couldn't erase everything his father had said from his mind.

It was unbelievable. Ken had become the model son over the last few weeks, but it didn't matter one bit. In his father's eyes he'd always be a distant second to Will Simmons.

When Jeremy arrived at home on Tuesday evening, he was welcomed by the sounds of cheerful voices, laughter, and the clanging of dishes. He dragged his tired body toward the kitchen, psyched to see his father but also about ready to keel over. Maybe he could just beg out of dinner and hit the

67

sack. His mood didn't exactly meld with the chipper noises he was hearing anyway.

"Do they have cactuses in Arizona?" Jeremy heard his little sister Trisha ask.

"It's cacti, honey," his mother corrected lightly.

"What's cacti?" Trisha asked just as Jeremy entered the room. His father was sitting at the table with Trisha and Emma, looking tired and pale but alert. He had a glass of water in front of him along with five brown pill bottles of various sizes. Jeremy's eyes flicked away from the bottles the moment he felt them land there. He didn't want his father to see the concern on his face.

Jeremy's mother looked up from the pot of soup she was stirring on the stove. "Hi, Jeremy!" she said brightly.

"Hey," he said, smiling at his dad. "One cactus is a cactus, Trish," Jeremy explained, mussing her hair. "When you have more than one cactus, they're called cacti." He paused, glancing up at their mother. "But you know, I think it's okay to say cactuses, too," he pointed out. "I think you can use either word."

Trisha scrunched up her face and patted her brown hair back down into place. "I just want to know if they have them," she said, turning her attention to the coloring book that lay open in front of her on the table.

Jeremy and his father laughed, and Jeremy walked over to give his dad a quick hug. His father felt thin and frail under his sweatshirt, but Jeremy squelched the tickle of worry that ran down his spine. At least the color was back in his father's face. That was something.

"We were just talking about the big move," Jeremy's dad said as Jeremy lowered himself into a chair and picked up one of Trisha's crayons. "Trina called and said there would be no problem finding us a house. The market is great there right now."

Just what Jeremy wanted to hear. "Good," he said, peeling at the paper wrapper on the crayon.

"Jeremy! Don't!" Trisha scolded him. She grabbed the crayon out of his hand, and Jeremy started to drum his fingers on the table. If he was going to listen to Arizona talk, he had to have something to do with his hands or he was going to crawl out of his skin.

"Can we have a pool?" Emma asked, chewing on her hair like she always did when she was upset. Jeremy half smiled. Apparently he wasn't the only one stressed about the move.

"I don't see why not," his father said with a wink and a smile. "I'm sure there are lots of houses with pools in Arizona. What do you think, Jeremy? Think you could handle having a pool?"

Jeremy forced a smile. He knew what his dad was doing—trying to get him psyched about the move. It was a valiant effort, but a pool wasn't exactly going to take the place of Jessica and his friends and the chance to be the captain of his basketball team. "Yeah, Dad," Jeremy said. "A pool would be great."

"Can we have a slide into it like Jenny does?" Trisha asked, her eyes wide.

"Sure!" Jeremy's father exclaimed. He reached over and tousled Trisha's hair just as Jeremy had. Trisha sighed, shook her head, then patted her hair back into place once more. Jeremy smirked.

"Howard, you can't promise all that," Mrs. Aames hissed. "We haven't even seen the faxes from the realtor yet."

"Margaret, if I'm going to take my kids away from the ocean, I can at least give them a pool," Jeremy's father answered good-naturedly. "And if there's not a slide, we'll just have to put one in, won't we?"

"Yeah!" Trisha exclaimed.

Jeremy's mom rolled her eyes, but she smiled. As they continued to discuss details, Jeremy found himself tuning them out. All he could think about was Jessica. She'd been so hurt, it made him want to tear his heart out just thinking about it. He knew that the picture of her stricken face was going to be painted on his memory forever. How was he going to leave her? He'd loved her for so long—since the moment he'd met her, practically. He had no idea how he was going to say good-bye.

And then there was the basketball team—they had a real shot at states this year, and he would be the captain. And his friends . . .

Jeremy looked up at his parents as they continued to talk, trying to gauge their moods. They seemed to be in a jovial state of mind, bantering back and forth about what they could and couldn't live without. How would they take it if he asked them about Trent's idea? Would they be receptive, or would his father have another heart attack right there at the table?

Jeremy studied his dad's face—the familiar lines and wrinkles that had recently been joined by a few new ones. He might be weak, but he wasn't going to drop out of his chair just because Jeremy wanted to discuss something.

"I wonder what the high school is like out there," his mother said, breaking into his thoughts. "Big Mesa is really advanced, Jeremy. I'll bet you'll be way ahead of your new classmates."

"Actually, I wanted to talk to you about that," Jeremy said. He pushed his back against the chair and sat up straight. His parents both glanced at him, then at each other, curious. "What if I . . . what if I stayed here to finish out my senior year?"

Jeremy's mother slowly lowered the wooden spoon she was holding, the color draining from her face. "What?"

"Trent offered to let me stay with his family for the rest of the year so I could graduate with my class," Jeremy rushed ahead, gripping his hands together under the table. "I could play on the team and go to my prom and everything. And then when school's over, I could come out to Arizona."

"Jeremy—"

"Mom, it's just a few months," Jeremy interrupted. He heard the desperate tone of his voice and took a deep breath. "Please," he said. This had to work. It just had to. The more he thought about it, the more the idea of leaving panicked him.

"Jeremy, the family has to stick together right now," his mother said, forcing calmness. She shot a look at her husband, and Jeremy glanced at his dad. His color was a lot less robust now. Jeremy swallowed hard as his dad geared up to speak.

"Well, Margaret, let's just—"

"No. This is not up for discussion," Jeremy's mom interrupted firmly. She walked over to the table and looked Jeremy sternly in the eye. "This family has to stick together right now, and that's all there is to it. Now, you were going to have to leave your friends soon anyway, to go to college. It's just going to have to happen a little bit earlier, that's all."

He could tell his mom was dead serious, but Jeremy still had some fight in him. One last glance at his father, though, told him to keep his mouth shut. If this one short conversation could make him look that much weaker, Jeremy could imagine what a drawn-out debate would do.

Jeremy was just going to have to accept it. He was leaving California. And there was nothing he could do about it.

# Maria Slater

You know what? Ken's dad has just gotten on my last nerve. I'm sorry. I've always tried to give the man a little bit of rope because I know we're different, but I'm done. I just got off the phone with Ken, and I had to restrain myself from marching over to his house to slap some sense into his father. But I know that wouldn't help anything. And besides, the guy _is_ a lot bigger than me.

Still, how could he not realize how lucky he is to have a son like Ken? The kid _could_ be out there doing drugs or scamming girls or flunking out of school. But he's not. He's a model student, he doesn't even drink, and he has me! (I mean, could you _ask_ for a more perfect girlfriend? Hee hee.) Anyway, Ken was really upset by what his father said to him, and I don't get it. Why does Mr. Matthews feel the need to keep him at arm's length all the time? Is he just that heartless?

Well, I guess one good thing may come out of all of this. Ken will sure have a lot of pent-up aggression to take out on the football field this weekend.

# CHAPTER
## Unreasonable Hope

**6**

"So I e-mailed Ronde last night and told him about the plan, and he says he's cool with you taking his room as long as you don't touch his baseball-card collection," Trent said as he and Jeremy made their way down the hall on Wednesday morning. "Like you really care about his Mattingly rookie card . . . although if we hocked it, we could probably pay for the entire prom."

Jeremy tried to smile. "Seriously," he said, looking around at the familiar walls and posters and lockers that lined the hallway. All he could think about was how in a few weeks he was never going to see this place again—no matter how hard Trent tried to find a way to keep him here. He couldn't believe how rigid his mom had been about the idea of Jeremy staying with Trent. Sure, she had a right to be surprised, upset, angry, even. But couldn't she at least think about it?

They stopped at Trent's locker, and Trent continued

to jabber on as he went through his things. "I wanted to get both my parents together to ask them, but my mom's been completely zoned lately with this whole gala thing she's planning at the country club. She's pretty much never around, but I swear I'll ask them today."

"Cool," Jeremy said, leaning against the wall and tipping back his head. He knew he should tell Trent not to bother. There was no way his parents were going to let him stay in Big Mesa. His mother had made that fact painfully clear last night. But he couldn't bring himself to say the words. A small part of him was hanging on to the unreasonable hope that the whole thing would work itself out.

"You okay, man?" Trent asked. He glanced up at Jeremy as he loaded up his backpack with what seemed like half the contents of his locker. "You seem a little out of it."

"I'm fine," Jeremy answered, unable to make himself sound it.

"You should be better than fine!" Trent exclaimed, whacking Jeremy's shoulder with the back of his hand, then zipping up his bag. "Dude, I cannot wait until you move in. It's gonna be so killer. My mom loves you so much, I'll bet she'll let us get away with anything. I envision a lot of pizza in our future, my friend." Jeremy clutched the strap on his backpack as Trent babbled on excitedly about him and Jeremy being roommates. The more psyched Trent got, the further Jeremy seemed to slip into total depression. This was not going to happen. Very soon Jeremy was going to be alone, friendless and girlfriendless in the middle of the desert. The thought of all that emptiness made Jeremy want to clamp his hand over Trent's mouth just to make him stop talking. He couldn't handle hearing any more about all the fun he wasn't going to have.

"All right," Trent said with a determined nod, as if someone had just asked him a question. "I'm definitely asking them today."

"You know what? Forget it," Jeremy snapped, pushing himself away from the wall.

Trent's face fell. "What do you mean, forget it?" he asked, obviously stricken. Jeremy hardly ever snapped or raised his voice.

"I mean . . . just drop it, okay? I can't deal with this right now," Jeremy said, curtailing his frustration enough to lower his voice. Still, he was too tense to stick around and explain his outburst to Trent. He just had to get out of there before he lost it completely. "I gotta go," Jeremy said. And before Trent could say anything else, Jeremy lost himself in the sea of bodies making their way to second period.

*    *    *

"Ken! Get in here!" Coach Riley bellowed into the locker room on Wednesday afternoon. Ken's heart seized up in his chest as he laced up the front of his shoulder pads. He and Todd shot each other worried looks. Practice hadn't even started yet, and already he was going to get bawled out? Just what he needed.

Ken pulled his pads back off over his head and yanked on his T-shirt, ignoring the sympathetic glances of his teammates as he trudged by. Part of him just wanted to stroll out of the locker room at that moment and never look back, but Ken's days of turning his back on his problems were over—at school at least. Home was another story.

Pushing open the door to Riley's office, Ken swallowed hard and prepared himself for the torrent of insults he was undoubtedly about to endure. Who knew, maybe listening to Riley rail on him for a few minutes would get him psyched up for practice and the team wouldn't end up doing laps again.

Coach Riley was standing in the middle of his office, his hands on his hips. His shiny red nylon jacket was riding up to his stomach and bunched up on his arms, and his new baseball cap was so stiff, it made his forehead look about twice as long as it was. How could someone look so ridiculous and so intimidating at the same time? Coach was staring down at something on his desk, and when he lifted his eyes to meet Ken's, Ken held his breath and tried to meet his gaze head-on.

"Well, Ken," Riley said with a smile. Wait. A smile? "There's someone on the phone for you. I think you'll want to talk to him." He paused. "It's Hank Krubowski, from Michigan." Ken's jaw went slack, and the rest of his body seemed to want to go with it. "Don't just stand there like an idiot, Matthews, pick up the phone," Riley ordered.

Ken wiped his palms on his football pants and shakily reached to pick up the receiver, wishing he had time to process this information before he was forced to try to make conversation. But with Riley hovering over him, he was better off doing as he was told.

"Hello?" he said into the phone. Silence. He glanced at Riley, confused.

"You've gotta hit the button first, son," Riley said with an amused shake of his head. The coach reached out and pressed the little blinking hold button, and Ken blushed. Duh.

"Hello?" he tried again.

"Ken? This is Hank Krubowski from Michigan," a gruff voice barked. "How's the arm, kid?" he asked.

"Uh . . . fine," Ken said, self-consciously rolling back his throwing shoulder. Riley shot him an encouraging look, and Ken stood up a little straighter. "I mean, it's great, Mr. Krubowski. Couldn't be better."

"Good to hear, Matthews, 'cause I've got some good news." The guy cleared his throat loudly and coughed a few times. "Very good news."

Ken's heart was slamming so hard against his rib cage, he was sure the scout could hear it on the other end of the line. "Really?" he asked, squeezing his eyes shut when he heard himself sounding like an eight-year-old.

"Yep, things are looking good for you on my end," Krubowski responded. Ken heard the sound of shuffling papers in the background. "You perform at your game this weekend and I think I can secure a solid scholarship for you, Ken."

"Really?" Ken said again, glancing over at Riley, who looked like he was just about salivating to hear what was being said on the phone line. "I mean, thank you."

"No, thank you, Ken," Krubowski said. "Michigan can use a few more guys like you on our team."

"Thanks," Ken said, feeling a wave of relief wash through him. "You won't be disappointed."

"I'm sure I won't be," Krubowski said with a small laugh. "I'll see you this weekend, Ken."

"Great. Bye!" Ken said, but Krubowski had

already hung up. Ken stood there for a split second, listening to the dead line and savoring the moment. A scholarship—to Michigan! After everything he'd gone through the past couple of days—the doubts, the fear, the stress . . . his father—he couldn't imagine anything more perfect than the brief conversation he'd just had. All his dreams were about to come true.

It was all up to him.

"Wanna go to the Gap?" Tia asked Jessica on Wednesday afternoon as they walked through the mall with Elizabeth and Maria. She twirled around, checking out the stores on either side of them, obviously trying to find something to tempt Jessica out of the funk she was in. Jessica, however, was in such heavy wallowing mode, she wasn't sure she'd ever want to come out, as much as she appreciated Tia for trying. "Jess?" Tia said, raising her eyebrows. "Gap?"

"Nah," Jessica said, staring straight ahead.

"BCBG?" Elizabeth suggested.

"Nah," Jessica repeated.

"How about Banana?" Maria put in, pointing at the store as they strolled by.

"Nah."

Tia stopped in her tracks and narrowed her eyes

at Jessica. "Want to go jump in the fountain and gather pennies and use them to buy corn dogs?"

"Nah," Jessica said tonelessly, continuing to walk even though all her friends had stopped. A few steps later Jessica realized a distinct lack of conversation around her and looked around in confusion. "What are you guys doing?" she asked when she spotted the three of them standing twenty paces behind her.

"Waiting for you to snap out of it," Maria said, placing her hands on the hips of her multicolored striped skirt.

Jessica shook her head to try to clear it as her friends caught up with her. "Sorry," she said. "I guess I'm just a little out of it."

"No kidding," Elizabeth said, slinging her arm around her sister's shoulders. "I've been a little worried about you ever since you poured syrup on your English muffin this morning."

"Um, ew?" Tia said, scrunching up her little nose.

Jessica snorted a laugh and put her arm around Elizabeth's waist. "You know what, guys, I appreciate what you're trying to do, but I don't think the mall is going to help me forget the fact that Jeremy's moving." Just saying the words made her heart pang painfully.

"This is serious," Maria said. She pulled a pack of gum out of her purse and held it out to her friends. Elizabeth and Tia each took a piece, but Jessica just stared at it as if she didn't know what it was, and Maria tossed the pack back into her bag. "Okay, if shopping and Cinnaburst aren't going to cheer the girl up, I say we just have her committed now."

Elizabeth smiled and rubbed Jessica's back. "Isn't there anything we can do?"

"You could grab Jeremy and hold him captive in the basement until his parents are long gone," Jessica said with a weak smile. "I'll take care of him, I swear."

"Right," Elizabeth said, rolling her eyes. "Tell that to all the other pets you've starved, lost, or set free."

"Well, speak of the devil," Tia said, looking past Jessica down the concourse as she snapped her gum.

"Jeremy?" Jessica asked, whirling around so fast, she whacked Elizabeth with the back of her hand.

"Nope. Just his second in command," Tia joked, barely covering the tension in her voice. Then Jessica spotted the reason for her friend's discomfort. Trent Maynor was making his way up the steps toward them, and he grinned and waved when Jessica made eye contact. Jessica wondered if this was the first time Tia had run into him since their brief dating thing back when Angel had just left for college. Tia had never shared the gory details, but Jessica knew that it had all pretty much blown up in her face when Trent discovered that Tia and Angel hadn't actually broken up yet at the time.

"You okay?" Jessica asked Tia under her breath as Trent approached.

"Me? Fine!" Tia said, reaching up to twirl a thick chunk of hair around her finger and blowing a bubble so big, it almost covered her entire face.

"Ladies!" Trent said, striding up to them. "What brings you to the mall on this fine day?" He looked over at Tia and knitted his brow, then reached up and popped her bubble with his pointer finger.

"Uh, shopping?" Tia joked as her bubble deflated and hung over her chin.

"Very smooth," Trent said with a sly smile. Tia laughed as any tension in the air melted away. "So, Jess," he continued, turning to her. "You should call Jeremy. He was really out of it at school today." He snapped his fingers distractedly. The guy was always so bursting with energy, he seemed to be in a constant state of fidget.

"No wonder, with everything that's going on," Elizabeth said. She pulled her white denim jacket closer to her body and hugged it there.

"Is he okay?" Jessica asked. She wished her

parents would cave and let her get a cell phone. She'd be on the line to Jeremy right now.

"I don't know," Trent answered with a shrug. "I thought my offer to stay with my family for the next few months would have chilled him out a little, but today he seemed even more freaked than he did yesterday."

Jessica's breath caught in her throat, and she glanced at Elizabeth, confused. Had she just heard right? Trent had asked Jeremy to *stay* with him? This was news to her.

"Wait a second, you mean Jeremy can stay with you until the end of the year?" Jessica asked. "He can *do* that?"

"Well, I wasn't sure until just now," Trent said, leaning back against the little wall that separated shoppers from the open atrium. He looked over his shoulder down at the first floor. "I finally asked my dad, and he had no problem with it, and he doesn't think my mom will either." Trent's brow wrinkled, and he seemed to realize something. "Wait, you mean he didn't tell you?" he asked, glancing back at Jessica.

"No," Jessica said numbly.

"Maybe it slipped his mind," Maria said, not even sounding convinced herself. It was kind of a big piece of news to have slipped his mind.

"Yeah, maybe," Jessica agreed, trying to sound normal even though her head was spinning. There was a possibility that Jeremy could stay in California, and he hadn't even told her? That could only mean one thing—he wasn't even considering it. How could this be? And how could he not even *talk* to her about it?

# Will Simmons

Ken's going to get a scholarship to Michigan. <u>My</u> scholarship. The one that Hank Krubowski had basically handed to me until I wrecked my leg.

I can't believe this. I can't <u>believe</u> this. Josh told me it was all anyone was talking about this afternoon— how Riley and Ken were in Riley's office on the phone with Krubowski and how Ken came out all high on himself. Unbelievable. I was scouted by Michigan. They wanted <u>me</u>. Ken never even got in the game until I got injured.

Why did this have to happen? Why now, when I was just starting to feel like I was getting over it? I mean, yeah, I have to get through championship week, but once that's done, the season is over. After Friday (and however long it takes everyone to stop talking about the game _after_ it's played), I wasn't ever going to have to think about Ken Matthews and everything he has again. But now it's going to be with me the rest of the year. He'll probably start wearing Michigan sweatshirts and walking around school talking about all the incentives they're throwing at him.

Why did it have to be Michigan?

Well, I guess they don't mind taking sloppy seconds.

Life sucks.

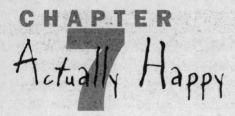

# Actually Happy

"I can't believe I'm doing this," Alanna said, holding her hand over her mouth to hide her ridiculously wide grin. Conner couldn't get over the size of the dimples that formed in her cheeks every time she so much as smirked.

"I can't believe you've never done it before," Conner said. He picked up the little rubber mallet, placed a mangy foam-rubber frog on the minicatapult, and concentrated. In front of him dozens of little lily pads were circling the water. "The key to this game is timing," he told Alanna as a loud victory bell sounded from a game somewhere else on the boardwalk, followed by the overly excited cheers of the winner. He held the mallet above the little round lever and brought it down as hard as he could, sending the foam-rubber frog flying with an impressive trajectory. So impressive, it sailed over the makeshift pond and landed on the ground on the other side.

"Timing, huh?" Alanna asked with a laugh. "You

don't know your own strength." She grabbed the mallet out of Conner's hand. "Let me try."

Conner placed a new frog on the catapult and took a step back. "Be my guest," he said. He watched as Alanna's face scrunched in concentration, her frizzy brown curls blowing wildly around in the breeze coming off the water. Coming to the boardwalk had been a brilliant brainstorm, and Conner gave himself a mental pat on the back for thinking up the idea. No one could be depressed or bored with all of this colorful cheesiness surrounding them. "Um, Alanna? Are you going to do this anytime today?" Conner asked.

At that moment Alanna brought down the mallet and the frog tumbled through the air, landing ungracefully with three limbs in a lily pad and one limb out. Conner's eyes widened. She'd done it.

"Yes!" Alanna screamed, jumping into his arms. "I rule the frog game! What do I win? What do I win?" she asked, looking around at the rows and rows of prizes while keeping one arm hooked around Conner's neck.

"Great," Conner said. "Does this mean I have to carry around one of those huge stuffed animals now?"

"The hugest one I can find," Alanna said, her gray eyes sparkling. Conner shook his head as Alanna carefully weighed the pros and cons of the hundred different, brightly colored stuffed dogs hanging above their heads. She finally picked a shocking pink one that had a huge blue tongue hanging out of its mouth. The pimply faced kid working the frog game knocked the dog down into her arms, and Alanna held it out, gazing at it with pride.

"If you're gonna be cheesy, might as well go all the way," she said, shoving the dog into Conner's arms. "I think I'll name it Mac, after you."

"Yeah, great," he said sarcastically. But he couldn't stop himself from smiling. As they walked along the creaky planks past hot-dog stands, roulette wheels, and photo booths, Conner was fairly certain he'd never been this happy. Everything seemed to be falling into place all at once—something he would have previously thought impossible. Things were going great at home—both his mother and Megan seemed happy and healthy and were hardly ever on his case anymore. His guitar lessons were getting more and more intense, and Conner really felt like he was improving. And to top it all off, he had Alanna—the one person who intrigued him, made him laugh, and accepted him with all his faults.

Unlike Elizabeth.

"I think I could live on cotton candy alone," Alanna said as she stopped to watch the lady behind the cotton-candy counter roll a big wad of the pink fluffy stuff onto a paper cone. Conner smiled. It was tough sometimes, seeing Elizabeth at school and not being able to talk to her or hold her. Even Conner could admit that he and Elizabeth had shared something . . . unique. But that part of his life was over now. He was moving on. And there was no one better—or more different from Elizabeth—to do it with than Alanna.

"Can we get one large?" Conner asked the cotton-candy lady, pulling out his wallet.

Alanna grinned at him. "Aw, you spoil me," she teased.

"Nah, I just want to see what you're like all hopped up on sugar," Conner said matter-of-factly. He took his change and stuffed his wallet back into his back pocket, balancing the big pink dog on his knee the entire time. He imagined what he must look like at that moment and let out a quick laugh. "I hope you know that if anyone asks me if I was here this afternoon, I'm denying everything," he said.

"I would hope so," Alanna shot back. "Let's go sit while I eat this." She pulled a wad of cotton candy from the cone and sucked it off her index finger as she headed for a nearby bench. They settled in together right across from the dart game, where three guys clad in black leather jackets were arguing with each other over how to win.

Conner's brow furrowed as he watched the biggest of the three—a bald guy with a long goatee—shove one of his friends.

"You're such an idiot, Wade," he yelled. "This is a total setup."

Wade shoved back, and it looked like the two were about to go at it when the third guy stepped in. This one was totally shaky on his feet, and it was clear to Conner that he was on something, but he didn't know what until the guy pulled a flask from his jeans and took a long swig, then offered it to his buddies.

"Look at these morons," Conner said, his jaw clenching as his eyes shot to the frightened girl who was manning the booth. "They're trashed."

Alanna suddenly looked sick to her stomach, and she stopped working on her cotton candy. "God," she said quietly. "In the middle of the afternoon."

The shouting escalated, and for a minute Conner thought he was going to have to step in, but then a couple of security guys arrived and broke it up. Conner let out a little sigh of relief.

"I am never touching that stuff again," he said, leaning back into the rickety bench. "Those guys are so pathetic." *And I was just like them,* he added inwardly.

Alanna was silent, and Conner realized that he was waiting for her to say something—to agree with him in some way. When she said nothing, he felt his heart take a little skip of warning. Was Alanna thinking about drinking again? Or worse yet—had she already started up?

She shifted in her seat, and Conner felt himself freeze, waiting for the worst.

"I can't even *imagine* ever drinking again," she said finally, causing Conner to sag with relief. As much as he wanted to be with Alanna, he didn't know what he'd do if he found out she was hitting the bottle. He liked her a lot, but he wasn't an idiot. No matter how much fun they had together, going out with someone who was still drinking would be seriously bad news.

"*Tribune* sports desk, can I help you?" Will asked. He waited as the caller barked a request, then hit the four-digit extension and the transfer button and hung up. Then he rolled in his chair over to the fax machine, stuffed in a fax, and dialed the number. The phone rang again, and he wheeled back, grabbing the receiver just as Dan Murphy, a senior editor, dropped a FedEx on the desk for Will to send out.

"ASAP," Murphy said as Will picked up the phone.

"Got it," Will answered, holding his hand over

the mouthpiece. Then he pulled it away and said in his best all-business voice, "*Tribune* sports desk, can I help you?"

Once that call was transferred, Will filled out the FedEx form, dropped it at the mail room, and picked up his sent fax on the way back to the front desk. By the time he sank back into his chair, he was feeling very satisfied with himself. Who knew he'd be so good at . . . what was it called again? Multitasking! In the last fifteen minutes he'd done more than he had all day at school.

"Look at everything I've done already," Will said to himself, nodding proudly as he surveyed his domain. And he hadn't once thought about how jealous he was of Ken all afternoon. This job was the best thing that could have happened to him. Will was just about to make a celebratory trip to the break room to snag a couple of Twinkies out of the vending machine when the phone rang again and he grabbed it.

"*Tribune* sports desk, can I help you?" he asked.

"Yeah, this is Hank Krubowski for Ed Matthews," a gruff voice spat. Will's blood instantly ran cold. Hank Krubowski. As in . . .

"Can I ask what this is regarding?" Will asked, knowing perfectly well what the answer would be.

"I'm calling from the University of Michigan,"

Krubowski said, his tone still sour. "Is he there or not?"

Exactly. Hank Krubowski. As in the guy who had scouted Will at the beginning of the year. The guy who'd taken him and his parents and Melissa out to brunch because he wanted to sign Will so badly. The guy who hadn't so much as called when Will had gotten hurt. The guy . . . who was now getting seriously impatient on the other end of the line.

"One moment, please," Will said, hitting the hold button as he tried to catch his breath. What was Krubowski doing calling Ken's dad at work? Was he going to make an offer? But that wasn't the way it usually happened. The coach usually met with the player *and* his family. And according to Josh's rumor mill, that wasn't going to happen until after the championship game.

"Hey, Will," Mr. Matthews said, striding by the desk.

"Oh! Mr. Matthews!" Will said, snapping out of his daze. He held up the phone. "There's a Hank Krubowski on the phone for you."

Mr. Matthews stopped in his tracks and turned to look at Will, who could have sworn that Mr. Matthews looked flushed. "Oh . . . I'll . . ." Mr. Matthews looked around for a second as if he couldn't recall where he was. "I'll take it in there," he said, pointing at the conference room.

"No problem," Will said as Mr. Matthews went inside and closed the door behind him. He shakily looked up the extension number for the conference room and punched it in. Once the call was successfully transferred, he sat there frozen, staring at the little red light that indicated the conference-room phone was in use. Will knew after reading the manual that he could listen in on the call if he hit mute and picked up the line. For one irrational second he actually considered it, but he couldn't bring himself to pick up the phone.

He spun around in his chair to face the filing cabinets behind him so he wouldn't have to look at the little light, but he couldn't stop thinking about Mr. Matthews's face when he'd heard who was on the phone. Something was going on here. And Will was going to go crazy until he figured out what it was.

"Jeremy! Jessica's here!" Mrs. Aames called up the stairs at Jeremy's house on Wednesday evening. Jessica stood at the bottom of the staircase with her, trying not to look as angry and upset as she felt, until Jeremy appeared at the top of the stairs.

"Hey!" Jeremy said, his face lighting up at the sight of her. Jessica felt heartsick, knowing that soon she wouldn't be able to see that reaction on his face anymore, but she tried to squelch her nostalgia. She had to remember that she was mad at him. "Come on up," Jeremy added.

"Thanks, Mrs. Aames," Jessica said, forcing a smile. Then she shoved her hands into the pockets of her denim jacket and stomped up the stairs.

"Come over to surprise me?" Jeremy asked as he walked back into his room with Jessica at his heels. He reached out to put his arms around her, but Jessica slipped right past him so that his fingertips merely brushed her arm.

"I was the one who was surprised this afternoon," Jessica said, an edge in her voice. She walked into the middle of the room and turned to face Jeremy, her eyes flashing. Jeremy took one look at her and his face fell. He slowly lowered himself onto his plaid bedspread and looked up into her eyes.

"What did I do?" he asked, resigned.

"Trent told me about his plan to have you move in with him," Jessica said, letting the words snap from her tongue. She knew she sounded a bit childish, but she couldn't help it. She sort of felt like she was being treated like a child. "What I can't figure out is why you didn't tell me. I mean, do you *want* to move? Do I even matter to you?"

"I don't believe this," Jeremy said quietly, shaking his head.

"What?" Jessica spat. How could he just dismiss her feelings like that? It was like he didn't even realize that the fact he was leaving was going to affect her too. Or he didn't care.

"I said, I don't believe this," Jeremy repeated, standing up. Now *his* eyes flashed, and Jessica could hear the frustration in his voice. "We've been over this a million times!" he said. "We just finished fighting over all that college stuff, and I thought you understood that you matter. What am I going to have to do to prove to you how much you mean to me, Jess?"

*Stay,* a little voice in Jessica's head whined. But she knew better than to say it out loud.

Jeremy took a deep breath and let it out slowly, rubbing his hand at the back of his neck. He walked over to Jessica and took her hands in his. Jessica felt a shiver travel up one arm, across her back, and down the other. She couldn't look Jeremy in the eye. It was too hard. So she just looked at their hands.

"Jess, telling you about the move almost killed me, okay?" Jeremy said softly. "And I didn't mention the possibility of staying because I didn't want to give you false hope. I knew that no matter what Trent and his parents said, it wasn't going to work out. But still, when I left you yesterday, I couldn't even think about moving, so I asked my parents about Trent's offer anyway."

"They said no?" Jessica asked meekly, feeling more than a twinge of guilt as she realized that Jeremy had only been trying to protect her. He was right—she was always so quick to doubt him, and he was never doing anything but putting her first.

"My father was really upset, and my mother put her foot down," Jeremy admitted. Tears sprang to Jessica's eyes. Up until that moment she'd been holding out hope that Jeremy might still be able to stay, but if his parents were going to be unreasonable . . . Jeremy lifted her chin with one finger and forced her to look at him through her watery eyes. "And she's right, Jessica," he said. "I have to be with my family. I can't leave them."

Jessica sniffled loudly. "I know," she said, heartbroken all over again. "I'm sorry. I didn't mean to put more pressure on you. And I'm sorry I jumped to the wrong conclusions."

Jeremy shrugged, a small smile crossing his lips. "Yeah, I'm used to it," he teased.

Jessica whacked him on the arm. "Jerk," she said, cracking a grin.

Jeremy pulled her into his arms, and they stayed there for a long time in the middle of his room, holding on to each other. Jessica felt that if she pulled away, her heart would stay stuck to Jeremy, leaving a gaping hole in the middle of her chest. At that moment she realized that saying good-bye to him was going to be the worst moment of her entire life.

# Conner McDermott

It's no secret that I've never been quick to trust people. It even took me a while to trust Alanna, which is why I went off on her about her parents before taking five seconds to think about how illogical that was.

But when I really think about it, Alanna's the only person in this world I really should trust. Aside from Megan and my mother. And even that took me a long time to realize.

Alanna is the only person I know who has been through the same stuff I've been through. Obuiously we didn't have the exact same experiences, but close enough. And because of that, I know I can believe whatever she says.

Once you know that, what else is there?

# CHAPTER
## Serious Thought

8

"I'll get it," Jeremy said when the phone rang in the middle of dinner on Wednesday evening. It was, in fact, a relief to get up from the table, considering how tense and silent it had been since his family had sat down for the meal. Even though he knew it was immature, Jeremy didn't feel like speaking to his parents, and it seemed like they felt the same way. The girls were picking up on the vibe and had spent the last few minutes staring down at their food and pushing their vegetables around on their plates.

"Tell whoever it is we're eating," his mother told him, just like she did every single time the phone rang during dinner.

*I wouldn't exactly call it that,* Jeremy thought as he jogged into the kitchen and grabbed the portable. He hadn't swallowed more than three bites of food, and he was sure no one else had eaten much more. "Hello?" he said into the phone.

"Hey, J.!" Trent's voice said cheerily. "I just talked

to my mom, and you are now officially invited to stay with us for the rest of the year."

All of Jeremy's insides seemed to turn to solid rock in a split second, and the small amount of chicken and mashed potatoes he'd just consumed seemed to ball up in his stomach. He felt like someone had just dangled the key to possible happiness in front of his face and then snatched it away.

"Dude, did you hear what I said?" Trent asked. "You're in!"

"Yeah," Jeremy answered, gripping the counter in front of him with his free hand. "I can't talk right now, T."

Trent snorted a laugh. "Wait a minute. I call you to tell you the biggest news ever, and you can't talk right now?" he asked incredulously. "What is with you, man?"

Jeremy squeezed his eyes shut and took a deep breath. It was time to level with Trent. "Listen, I appreciate the offer. I do," he said. "But I can't do it. I have to stick with my family."

"Oh, man! Come on!" Trent exclaimed. "They can do without their golden boy for a few months."

"I'm sorry, man, it's just not going to happen. But thank your parents for me," Jeremy said. He looked over his shoulder toward the dining room, which was still eerily quiet. His parents could probably hear every word he was saying. "I have to go, T. I'm eating dinner."

There was a long silence. Or long for Trent anyway. "All right, bro. I'll see you tomorrow."

"Yeah." Jeremy hung up the phone, leaned forward, and rested his head in his hands for a moment. He would have killed to have been able to say yes to Trent. Just knowing that it was really possible that he could stay made the reality of leaving about fifty times worse. But he had to keep his head up. He couldn't let his dad know how much this was affecting him.

By the time Jeremy returned to the table, he looked composed and perfectly normal. Or at least he hoped he did.

"What was that all about?" his mom asked as he took his seat next to her.

"Yeah, what was that all 'bout?" Trisha piped in.

Jeremy smiled. "It was Trent," he said, picking up his fork to mush up the mashed potatoes he was now definitely not going to finish. "He asked his parents about me staying, and they said yes."

The table fell silent again, and Jeremy watched his mother and father exchange a concerned glance. It wasn't like he was expecting them to change their minds, but he still felt disappointed when they didn't say anything.

"Don't worry, you guys. I told him no," Jeremy assured them. He took a sip of his water, still striving for normalcy, even though a little voice inside his head was screaming at him to tell them—tell them how much he wanted and needed to stay here. Tell them what their decision was doing to him. Instead he looked each of his parents in the eye and smiled.

"It's not even an issue anymore," he said. "I know I should be with you."

"Ken, calm down," Maria said with a laugh as Ken paced back and forth in front of the bay window in the living room of his house. "If you jump him the second he walks through the door, he's going to think you're some crazed lunatic burglar and lay you out."

"I can't help it," Ken said, glancing out the window when he saw a pair of headlights swing onto his street. He couldn't wait to tell his father about Krubowski's phone call that afternoon. Of course his dad had picked today to work late. Apparently Will Simmons hadn't done anything spectacular enough to merit Mr. Matthews running home from work to tell Ken all about it. Ken shook his head. No negative thoughts. This was his night, and he wasn't going to let thoughts of Will Simmons wreck it.

"You all right?" Maria asked, leaning forward in

the brown corduroy La-Z-Boy. She reached back to tighten the knot in the red-and-orange scarf she had tied around her head, watching him the entire time.

"I'm great," Ken said. He was just freaking out, that was all. "Wait! Here he is!"

His father's car pulled into the driveway, and it seemed like it took forever for the man to turn off the headlights and kill the engine. Finally Ken couldn't take it anymore. He opened the front door just as his father was getting out his keys.

"Hey, Dad!" Ken said, holding the door for him.

Ken's father was startled but recovered quickly. "Hello, son," he returned. He walked inside and hung his jacket on the pegs by the door. "Hello, Maria. What's with the greeter over here?" he asked her, pointing his thumb over his shoulder at Ken.

"He's just a little excited," Maria said good-naturedly, standing to greet Ken's dad.

"Really?" Mr. Matthews raised his eyebrows and turned back to Ken. "What's going on?"

"You're never gonna believe this, Dad," Ken said, rubbing his hands together. "Hank Krubowski called me today in Riley's office." He stopped to wait for his father to react, holding his breath as he watched his dad's face.

"And?" his father prompted him. Not much, but at least there was some excitement in his voice.

"*And* he said that if I play well this weekend, he'll be able to secure me a scholarship!" Ken announced, beaming.

His father's face lit up, and Ken had never felt so elated in his life. "Ken, that's great!" Mr. Matthews said. He leaned over and half hugged Ken, clapping him on the back a few times for good measure. "You deserve it, son."

Ken grinned as he stepped away from his father. There were four words he'd never thought he'd hear from the man. He glanced over at Maria, who looked as happy as he felt, and he knew she realized how much what his father had said meant to him.

"Thanks, Dad," Ken said. "And I know I can do it. I'm going to have the game of my life this weekend, and next year I'll be wearing the blue and gold." Even hearing himself say those words sent a shiver of excitement through Ken's chest.

"And I can't wait to see it," Mr. Matthews said. He looked from Ken to Maria and back again, his eyes shining with what could only be pride. Ken felt like this couldn't possibly be reality. He'd been excited to tell his father his news, but he'd never expected even this much emotion out of the man. "I think it's time for a celebration," Mr. Matthews said. "Who's up for root-beer floats?"

"I'm in!" Maria said, raising one hand in the air. She

grabbed Ken's arm and pulled him over to her. "I think that went well," she whispered as she and Ken followed his dad into the kitchen. "The guy's not *all* bad."

"Yeah, right," Ken shot back. But he couldn't stop smiling. There hadn't been one single mention of Will Simmons since his father walked through the door. And that was enough to keep Ken happy for the rest of the night.

Jeremy was kicking back on the leather couch in the living room, wearing his favorite pair of sweats and watching *The Godfather*, when his father walked in and cleared his throat. Jeremy almost winced but managed to control himself. The last thing he wanted to talk about at that moment was the move. All he wanted to do was immerse himself in the mobster world for a little while, recite lines from memory, and forget all about what was going on in real life.

"Can we talk?" his father asked.

Without looking up, Jeremy picked up the remote at his side and muted the television. His father took a few tentative steps into the room, and Jeremy reluctantly slid over on the couch to make space. He wasn't exactly angry at his father; he was just . . . irritated at the world.

"What's up?" Jeremy asked, crossing his arms over

his ratty old basketball T-shirt. His lucky basketball T-shirt. The one he wouldn't be wearing for luck again since he wouldn't be playing on the team anymore.

His father sighed loudly and let out a little grunt as he lowered himself onto the couch, which made a creaking sound as he sat. He turned a bit to face Jeremy and rubbed his hands on the thighs of his crisp khakis. His second day home from the hospital and already the guy was trying to dress the part of a perfectly healthy man. Jeremy was just a little depressed, and he had reverted directly to his most comfortable comfort clothes.

"Well, son," his father began. He paused and cleared his throat as if he was putting off saying what he had to say. "I hate to have to admit this, but I overheard a bit of your conversation with Jessica earlier."

Jeremy's face flushed, and his irritation quickly turned to anger. Funny how fast that could happen when he was hovering on the brink. "You were eavesdropping on me?" he demanded, looking at his father's weary face for the first time since he'd entered the room.

"No!" his father protested. Then he shook his head. "Not really. But the point is, I realized she must have a lot to do with the fact that you want to stay here." He smiled a sympathetic smile at Jeremy, his eyes softening. "It's clear how much you two mean to each other."

At his father's words the anger seemed to wash right out of Jeremy and was replaced by pure exhaustion. All he wanted was for someone to tell him what to do—tell him how to handle this situation so that no one would get hurt. But it seemed totally impossible.

"And I know how much your senior year means to you," his father continued, clasping his hands in front of him. "Most of it is still to come—your class trip, the prom, graduation, yearbooks. . . ."

"Dad, I'm sorry, but is there a point to this?" Jeremy asked, adjusting in his seat. He couldn't stand to have it driven home once again exactly how much he was going to miss.

"Sorry," his father said, smiling again. "The point is, I talked it over with your mother, and we've agreed to let you stay with Trent—if that's what you decide you want."

Jeremy waited for a moment as what his father had just said sank in. "Really?" he asked, holding off the pure rush of joy that was threatening to overcome him until he heard if there were any conditions to this monumental decision.

"The ball is in your court," his father said seriously. "It's all up to you."

Jeremy laughed and quickly hugged his father.

"Thanks, Dad," he said as his father clapped him on the back.

"I want you to think about it, though, Jeremy," his father said as they pulled away from each other. "I know you'll make the decision that's right for you, but just make sure you weigh everything first."

"I will," Jeremy said with a nod. His dad got up and left the room, but Jeremy barely noticed. He was already thinking ahead to calling Jessica and Trent and giving them the news. No. Not phone calls. He'd have to tell them in person. They were both going to freak out. He couldn't wait to see the look on Jessica's face—

"Jeremy?"

He looked up to find Emma and Trisha standing at the door to the living room in their pajamas. Emma was wearing the glasses she only wore after her contacts were out for the night, and Trisha's once braided hair was sticking out in all directions.

"What are you guys doing up?" Jeremy asked.

"She can't sleep," Emma said, rolling her eyes.

"Neither can you!" Trisha protested, pulling her favorite doll out from behind her back and hugging it to her chest.

Jeremy felt a little pang of sympathy in his heart. He knew his sisters were scared about the move. They'd never lived anywhere but Big Mesa, and the idea of new schools and new people was keeping their little brains wired at night.

"You guys wanna come join me?" he asked. He pressed stop on the DVD remote and switched over to the Cartoon Network, which was in the middle of a *Josie and the Pussycats* marathon.

"Yeah!" Trisha exclaimed, bounding across the hardwood floor and hurling herself into Jeremy's lap.

"Okay," Emma said nonchalantly, keeping up the I'm-too-cool-to-care act. She walked over and plopped down on Jeremy's other side.

He pulled the worn afghan his mom had made when he was born out from behind them and covered all three of them with it. His sisters cuddled up on either side of him and were asleep within five minutes. Jeremy sighed and ran his hand over Trisha's fine brown hair.

He'd been so excited to tell Jessica about his parents' decision just a few minutes ago, but could he really do it? Could he leave the sisters that so obviously needed him just for his own selfish reasons?

Jeremy's dad was right. He really was going to have to give this some serious thought.

# Alanna Feldman

I'm so relieved that Conner is sticking around in my life. I mean, I'm happy and everything, but more than that, I'm relieved. Since he showed up at my house yesterday, I haven't thought about drinking once. Conner makes me want to be a better person. Even if I did think about drinking, I wouldn't do it because I know he'd be disappointed in me. And it would kill me to know he was disappointed in me.

I just wonder if I should have told him about that drink I took yesterday. I've thought about telling him. I've thought about it a lot, actually. Not telling him almost feels like lying in a way. Like when we were at the boardwalk and we saw those guys and we both said we'd never drink again, I know Conner thought that I hadn't had a drink since before we were at the clinic. And I didn't correct him. So that feels like a lie.

The thing is, I don't know how Conner would react if he knew I'd had alcohol since we'd been home, but I have an idea. And I think he would leave me. I think he would decide I was weak and disgusting and stupid and he would leave me. And that would just make everything worse. So I have to keep on lying. Or at least, not sharing everything.

As long as I have Conner, I know I can get through this.

I'll do it for him.

# CHAPTER
## *Rash Decision*
**9**

Will lightly rapped on the open door to Mr. Matthews's office and peeked his head inside. Mr. Matthews was just getting up from his chair and shrugging into his Angels baseball jacket.

"You wanted to see me?" Will asked, hovering by the door respectfully.

"Yes! Come in! Come in!" Mr. Matthews said, gathering up some things and stuffing them into his battered backpack. That was one of the things Will really liked about Mr. Matthews—he wasn't some uptight guy who carried a briefcase and wore a suit jacket. He was a sports reporter, and he dressed like someone who had to spend a lot of time outdoors, running around from soccer field to lacrosse field to basketball court.

"Listen, Will, I hate to do this to you, but I really need someone to file all this stuff," Mr. Matthews said, gesturing at the teetering pile of papers in the out box on his desk. "I'm gonna be out of the office for the next few hours . . . would you mind?"

Will smiled. "Not at all," he said. At least filing in Mr. Matthews's office would keep him away from the sports desk and all the wacked demands of the other editors and writers. Earlier that afternoon someone had asked him to look up how many people with the last name Miller had made all-state teams in the last five years. What good could that information possibly do anyone?

"Great," Mr. Matthews said, pulling his backpack onto his shoulder. "The filing system is pretty self-explanatory, but anything you're unsure of, just set aside and we'll look at it later. Thanks again." With that, Mr. Matthews disappeared, obviously running late for some game or other.

Will stood still for a moment and took the time to really check out his surroundings. He'd been in this office plenty of times but had always avoided looking like he was too interested. He didn't want to be rude, gaping at all of the cool stuff Mr. Matthews had collected. But now he was really able to study everything—the walls decorated with pictures of Mr. Matthews shaking hands with random sports celebrities, the framed letters from high-school athletes thanking him for his coverage of their careers, the shelves of books by retired all-stars and coaches.

There were baseball cards, autographed balls, an Oakland Raiders helmet. Will smiled. He could really get used to a life where you were *required* to be obsessed with sports.

He picked up the pile of papers and slapped them down on top of one of the tall black file cabinets, then got to work. The files were divided by schools and then by athletes from those schools. It was fairly easy to figure out how to file the schedules, clippings, and letters. Will was breezing right along, thinking he might get himself a Snapple and relax for a couple of minutes after he was through filing, when he came across something odd.

It was a University of Michigan envelope that had been torn open roughly—there were shards of the envelope flap sticking out in all directions—and the letter had been stuffed back inside the envelope. Will glanced at the chicken-scratch handwriting above the Michigan logo. It read *H. Krubowski*. Will swallowed hard. This was weird. All the other papers in the pile had been removed from their envelopes and flattened out, ready for filing. This envelope looked like it had been tossed in the pile as an afterthought.

*Or to hide it,* Will thought. His heart was pounding. He glanced around as if someone might be watching him, but everyone outside the office was just rushing around, going about their business.

Before he even registered what he was doing, Will had pulled the letter out of the envelope and unfolded it in his shaking hands. It wasn't typed on Michigan stationery as Will expected but scrawled on a piece of yellow legal paper. This was just getting weirder and weirder. Will started to read.

*Dear Ed,*

"Ed?" Will said aloud. These two were on a first-name basis? He shook his head and told himself to chill. Maybe they were just old friends. That would explain everything. Will continued to scan the page, reading as quickly as possible.

*I've made all the arrangements on my end in good faith. I'm trusting that you'll carry out your end of the bargain. Let's meet up at halftime at the championship game and seal the deal. Looking forward to it. —Hank*

Will felt ill and excited all at once as sweat beads popped out along his hairline and palms. Could this possibly mean what he thought it meant? Were Krubowski and Mr. Matthews involved in some sort of deal to get Ken into Michigan? If there was something Mr. Matthews had to offer Hank Krubowski, it would certainly explain why Ken—a second-rate quarterback at best—was being considered for one of the best football programs in the country. And why Mr. Matthews had been so flustered when Krubowski had called him at the sports desk the day before.

Will shut the door to Mr. Matthews's office and grabbed the phone, quickly dialing Melissa's number with one hand as he clutched the letter in the other. He had to run this by someone else and make sure that he wasn't just imagining things.

"Hello?"

"Liss?" Will said. "You're never going to believe this."

"I thought you were at work," Melissa said.

"I *am*," Will responded. "And you'll never believe what I found. I think Ken's dad is bribing the Michigan scout."

There was a brief pause. "What proof do you have?" Melissa asked point-blank. Will blinked. She didn't even sound shocked after taking a second to process his words. But then again, it took a lot to shock Melissa.

"This letter," Will said, quickly reading her the contents. This time when he read it, however, he realized it was totally inconclusive. Someone who wasn't as invested in this situation as he was would probably never jump to the conclusion he had. Maybe this deal Krubowski was talking about had nothing to do with Ken.

"Will, you have to report this," Melissa said. There was a twinge of conspiratorial excitement in her voice.

"I don't know," Will answered as he stared down

at the letter, reading it over and over again.

"What do you mean, you don't know?" Melissa demanded. "You can get back at everybody—Ken, that skeevy Krubowski guy, Mr. Matthews—"

"That's the thing, Liss," Will said, suddenly regretting his rash decision to call her. Knowing Melissa, she was never going to let this subject drop. "I don't want to do anything to Mr. Matthews. He did get me this job, and he's been so cool—"

"Will—"

"And besides, it's totally normal for scouts to talk to players' parents," Will pointed out.

"Yeah, to *talk* to them, not to send them secret letters talking about deals and shady meetings," Melissa argued. "I really think you should use this, Will. I don't know about you, but I'm sick of seeing Ken walk around the school like he's God's gift to SVH."

Will sighed. "Listen, Liss, just don't say anything about this to anyone until I find out more, okay?"

"Fine," Melissa said. "I'll keep it quiet . . . for now."

"Ken, this place is so cool!" Maria whispered as they opened their menus at a new restaurant called Chi on Thursday evening. Ken grinned and watched Maria as she admired the fresh-cut flowers on the table and a cool ocean breeze tossed the little curls around her face. He was feeling pretty good—about his choice of restaurant, his awesome practice that afternoon, and his impending college football career. Everything was falling into place.

"Yeah, not bad," Ken said. He took a sip of water from a clear wineglass and munched on the ice. "Todd told me about it. He said we have to get the dumplings. Apparently he asked for six more to go when he left here last Friday night."

"Well, that's not much to go on," Maria said with a grin. She adjusted the strap on her colorful slip dress and leaned in to the table like she was about to tell a secret. "Todd used to get six extra orders of onion rings at the Dairi Burger," she whispered, making a disgusted face.

"You have a point," Ken said, laughing. He and Maria caught each other's eye, and Ken just held her gaze for a moment. Sometimes he was still amazed that Maria was with him—that she'd taken him back and that she'd ever started dating him in the first place. She was the most beautiful girl in school, and the smartest, and, as far as he was concerned, the only one who knew how to dress. Sometimes he really couldn't believe his luck.

"I propose a toast," Maria said, lifting her water glass. "To my man," she added, giggling. "Soon to be MVP of the state championship game, soon to be quarterback at the University of Michigan . . . and just the hottest guy around."

"I don't know about that," Ken scoffed, clinking glasses with her. "But I'll drink to it," he added. They both sipped their water, and then the waitress came to take their orders.

As Maria asked questions about various dishes, Ken leaned back in his chair and smiled. He couldn't get over the amount of confidence Maria had in him. *But you deserve it,* a little voice in his head told him, and Ken's smile broadened. He did deserve it. He was going to kick butt at the game tomorrow, and any critics he might still have would be silenced— especially when Hank Krubowski draped a blue-and-gold Michigan jersey around his shoulders.

Tomorrow night. He could practically taste it.

"Ah, this is just what I needed," Jeremy said, taking a deep breath of the salty air as he climbed out of Trent's car on Thursday night. When Stan had called him earlier and asked him to come hang with a few guys at Crescent Beach, Jeremy had almost turned him down. He was so depressed, confused, and generally harassed, he didn't feel up to a night of socializing, but Stan had managed to convince him that his buddies could take his mind off his troubles, and here he was. Already the sound of the waves was working its soothing magic on his nerves.

"Thanks for making me come, guys," Jeremy said, following Stan and Trent up the reed-covered dune that separated the parking lot from the beach.

Stan snorted a laugh. "Don't thank us yet," he said, reaching down to crack a few of the drying reeds in his huge hand as he walked through them.

"What do you . . ." But Jeremy trailed off because he suddenly saw what Stan meant. The little beach was packed with people. It wasn't a gathering of a few guys. Half his class seemed to be there, gathered around a smattering of tiny bonfires that dotted the sand.

"Hey, they're here!" someone shouted. Then the whole crowd looked up and yelled, "Surprise!"

"What did you do?" Jeremy asked, stunned motionless. The smell of barbecued chicken and roasting marshmallows wafted its way over to them on the sea breeze, and Jeremy could see cans of soda being passed around.

"Not much," Trent said with a grin as Jessica broke away from the crowd and jogged over to them. "Just threw together a little going-away extravaganza for you."

"Hey, guys!" Jessica said, giving Trent and Stan quick hugs before throwing her arms around Jeremy. "You never told me there were so many hot girls who love you at your school," she said with a grin. "There are *a lot* of girls here," she added. "Maybe it's a good thing you're moving to Arizona."

Jeremy smiled and kissed her. "There are girls at our school?" he joked, looking at Trent and Stan.

"Ha ha," Jessica said. She grabbed his hand and pulled him down the slope of sand and over to the crowd.

Everyone he knew was there—the football team, the basketball team, the cheerleaders, all the kids from his classes and clubs. Everyone came up to him in groups to tell him how much they were going to miss him and how school wouldn't be the same without him. Jeremy couldn't believe the turnout. Classmates came and went all the time. Did all of these people really care that he wasn't going to be around anymore?

"They like you. They *really* like you," Jessica teased, obviously noticing the stunned look on his face.

"Dude," Trent said, coming up behind him and slapping him on the back. "Doesn't matter where you go—we're always going to be your best friends."

"Yeah, you can't escape us," Stan added. Somehow he'd already found himself a stick with a toasted marshmallow on the end and was blowing on it to cool it off.

Jeremy grinned, his heart warming at his friends' words. "Oh, great. I thought I was getting away from you guys. What's the point of leaving?" he joked.

"Good! Then stay!" Trent exclaimed, throwing his arms out at his sides.

*If they only knew,* Jeremy thought. He hadn't told anyone about his parents' announcement that they would let him decide his fate. He wanted to make his decision first. That way if he decided to go, Jessica and the rest of his friends wouldn't feel like he was rejecting them. He knew that no matter how much he told them that it wasn't about them, they'd always feel let down if he made up his mind to go to Arizona.

"Hey, can I get some time alone with the man of the hour?" Jessica asked, lacing her fingers through his.

"Augh, this guy!" Trent said, rolling his eyes.

Jeremy grinned and shrugged. "Sorry, guys. Duty calls." He walked off with Jessica, leaving his friends to laugh and mock him behind his back. He knew they didn't actually care if he spent a few minutes alone with Jessica. It was just their job as guys to rib him for it.

"So, I just wanted to tell you that I'm going to miss you," Jessica said once they were a safe distance from the crowd. She laughed and pushed her hair away from her face. "As if you didn't already know that."

Jeremy squeezed her hand and stopped walking. "I know," he said, turning to face her. His heart felt like it was seizing up just from looking at her beautiful face in the moonlight. There was no one else in the world like Jessica Wakefield. How could he possibly let her go? "Trust me, I know," he added, leaning forward and putting his forehead to hers.

"Think long-distance relationships work?" she asked, closing her eyes.

"I think ours will," he answered.

She sighed, sounding relieved. "Good. Because we're always going to be together, no matter where we are," she said. "Your friends aren't the only ones you can't escape."

Jeremy pulled back and looked down into her clear, blue-green eyes. She meant it. This perfect, beautiful, popular, smart, unbelievable girl who could have any guy she wanted was going to stay with him even if he was miles away.

"I love you, Jessica," he said, practically choking out the words.

Her eyes immediately filled with tears, but she smiled. "I love you too, Jeremy."

# Jeremy Aames

### California pros:

I get to graduate with my class.

I get to live at Trent's, where they have 162 channels and a seemingly endless supply of pizza rolls.

I'll be captain of the basketball team, which, aside from the obvious benefits to my ego, will look really good to colleges.

I'll get to go on the senior ski trip and pull off the prank we've been planning since third grade (which I cannot write down due to the no-evidence rule).

I won't have to say good-bye to Jessica.

### Arizona pros:

I won't have to say good-bye to my family.

Plus, to be fair, the dry air might be good for my sinuses.

# CHAPTER 10
## Pride and Joy

When Alanna heard the door to her parents' room open on Friday night, her first instinct was to get up, haul her butt up the back stairs, and lock herself in her room, but she didn't move a muscle. She didn't even flinch before she realized it would be pointless. They would come find her wherever she was in the house. And she certainly didn't want it to look like they were getting to her.

Sure enough, moments after she first heard their footsteps on the stairs, her mother swept into the TV room, a whirl of mink coat and Chanel No. 5. Alanna didn't even look up. She could tell her mom was in the mood for a fight just by the chill in the air.

"Bert," her mother said loudly, staring at Alanna as if she'd addressed her daughter.

Alanna's father walked in and took his place next to his wife, gazing down his nose at Alanna. Her heart was pounding, but she didn't let it show. She never did. Why couldn't they just go out for the

131

night without lecturing her first? Did it give them the buzz they needed to tolerate their stuck-up so-called friends?

"What did I do now?" Alanna said lazily, watching the garish images of some random MTV special flick across the screen.

"It's more like what you're not doing," her mother said. "Isn't there some more useful way for you to spend your time?" She reached over, took the remote out of Alanna's hand, and snapped off the TV. Alanna was surprised her clueless mother so quickly knew which button to push.

"Such as?" Alanna said. She never took her eyes off the screen.

"Such as homework?" her father suggested.

Alanna finally glanced up at him, incredulous. "It's Friday night."

"Are you seriously trying to tell me that after a month of missed classes, you don't have enough work to keep you from the television?" he asked, arching his perfect eyebrows. Alanna sometimes wondered if her father got his naturally bushy brows waxed like her mother did—a fine use of *his* important time.

"Yes, that's what I'm telling you," Alanna said, choosing to forgo mention of the intimidating tower of assignments she had piled up on the never used desk in her room.

"Fine, then, what about some physical exercise?" her mother asked, perching on the edge of a chair. "I saw the Mastersons at the club this afternoon, and they tell me tennis tryouts are coming up. Missy could be all-state this year."

Alanna snorted. "Well, yippee for Missy."

"Wouldn't staying fit aid you in your . . . *rehabilitation?*" her mother asked, pronouncing the word *rehabilitation* as if it was something Alanna had just made up. Like a gibberish word that was almost beneath her mother's vocabulary.

Alanna's heart felt sick at the degradation of the ordeal she'd been through. She stood up on shaky legs.

"Like you really care about my rehabilitation," she spat, towering over her mother, whose face lost just a little bit of its color.

"Don't talk to your mother like that," her father ordered, taking a step toward her. "If we didn't care, why would we have sent you there in the first place? Why would we spend every other night enduring questions from our friends about where you were for a month?"

"So that's what this is really about," Alanna said with a bitter laugh. "Afraid your excuses aren't measuring up, Daddy? Afraid someone at the club might find out where your pride and joy really was last month?"

Her father pulled his face back slightly, almost imperceptibly, but it was enough for Alanna to know she had affected him. "Now, that's not fair . . . ," he began.

"And what is?" Alanna shouted. "Is the way you treat me fair? It's always the same thing. You want me to be someone I'm not. I'm never going to be Missy Masterson. I'm not a great student, and I suck at tennis. Why can't you just leave me alone?" she yelled, a tear spilling over. She wiped it away quickly and lifted her chin, trying for defiance but teetering on the edge of self-pity.

"Well, we tried that, didn't we?" her father said, yanking his driving gloves onto his hands. "And where did it get us?"

Alanna felt like she'd been slapped. Where did it get *them?* Was it always going to be about them?

"Come on, Phyllis. We're late." He swept out of the room without a second glance at Alanna or her mother.

Her mom rose from her chair and hesitated for just a moment, and Alanna sensed that she wanted to apologize. *Say something,* she willed her mother. *Say anything. Please.*

But her mother just tucked her chin and walked out. The moment Alanna heard the front door close, she burst into tears. The room blurred in front of her—the muted colors of the furniture melting into the dark-paneled walls. Alanna moved slowly out of the room, and before she knew what she was doing, she was in the den, standing in front of the liquor cabinet again, bawling her eyes out. It would be so easy. All she had to do was lift out the bottle of scotch, take it up to her room . . . and soon everything would be fine.

"No," Alanna said, turning her back on the cabinet. Instead she grabbed the phone and dialed Conner's number. He would help her get through this. He had to.

"And Sweet Valley High will start off with the ball on their own thirty-five yard line," the commentator announced as Ken and the rest of the offense took the field on Friday night. Ken jogged out to the center of the gridiron, keeping his shoulders back and his head up—the picture of confidence. No reason for the entire crowd to know that his nerves were jangling like a set of sleigh bells. The stands were packed to bursting, and all eyes were on him, but he knew the exact locations of only three people.

Maria was in the back of the stands with Elizabeth, Andy, and a bunch of other seniors.

His father was in the press box.

And Hank Krubowski was right on the sidelines, holding Ken's fate in his hands.

The team huddled up and Ken hunkered down, helmet to helmet with his teammates. "Okay, guys, we know what we have to do," he said, looking each of them in the eye. "One team's going home in body bags tonight, and it's not gonna be us." He earned some grunts of agreement and put his hand out into the center of the circle. "Wide right, thirty-two split on three, ready?" The rest of the guys put their hands in on top of his, and Ken yelled, "Break!" With that, they were off.

As Ken approached the line of scrimmage, he took a deep breath and blocked out all sounds, first the crowd, then the cheerleaders, then the voices of the opposing defense goading his teammates. He crouched behind his center, called the audible, and then the ball was in his hands and his cleats were digging into the soft dirt.

*Don't mess up. Don't mess up. Don't mess up.*

The offensive line was holding. He had plenty of time. No one was going to touch him. But there was no one open downfield. Ken's blood pressure skyrocketed. This couldn't happen. Not on the first play.

*Don't mess up. Don't mess up. Don't mess up.*

Ken pumped the ball, faking a pass to the left. Out of the corner of his eye he saw that the defender who was covering Todd took his bluff. He started to break left, and Ken let the ball fly. Todd made a beautiful catch, and the crowd went wild. By the time the cornerback realized his mistake and turned back, Todd was fifteen yards down the sideline. He was finally pushed out-of-bounds, but Ken had done his damage. He'd come out throwing and shown these guys they weren't going to scare him.

"A beautiful pass by number twenty-nine, Matthews, caught by number eighty-five, Wilkins, for a gain of thirty-three yards!" the announcer crowed. "It'll be first and ten, Gladiators on the Lions' thirty-two yard line."

Ken grinned as Todd jogged back to the line and pounded Ken on top of his helmet. "We're on our way!" Todd shouted.

"You know it!" Ken returned. Now he could finally relax. This game was his.


"Ring!" Alanna demanded, holding the portable phone out in front of her and glaring at the little gray buttons with everything she had in her. "Ring, dammit! Ring!"

She tossed the phone onto her bed, where it bounced, smacked against the headboard with a crack, and then landed on the carpet. Alanna started to pace, back and forth, back and forth, across the empty stretch of floor in the center of her bedroom—the few square feet that weren't covered by clothes, CD cases, and books. She clenched and unclenched her hands and tried to breathe normally, but nothing helped. She was so angry, so miserable, so tempted. She kicked a pile of jeans and sweaters aside and groaned. Why didn't he just call back?

Sitting down on the edge of her bed, Alanna dug her elbows into her thighs and pushed her head into her hands, staring down at her black socks. Conner hadn't been home. Megan had told her he was out, but he'd be home soon. How could he not be there? Where was he? Was he out with friends? With a girl? Was he out with some girl somewhere having a good time while she was trapped here in her room, rapidly losing her mind? What if he was with Elizabeth? What if he'd gone back to her after all?

Alanna looked up at her locked bedroom door. She'd forced herself to come up here to wait for his call, knowing that if she stayed in her father's study or if she stayed downstairs, for that matter, she'd be tempted to drink. And she didn't want to. Even if Conner *was* out with some other girl. Even if he wasn't there for her when she needed him most, that was no reason to go falling off the wagon.

*But you already did,* she reminded herself. Sure, it had been just a little bit and it had made her gag, but all it took was one sip to be considered a relapse.

*So if you already relapsed, what's the point of torturing yourself like this? What difference does it make? Just go downstairs. You'll feel so much better.* She could practically taste the warm liquid on her tongue. Feel it burning down her throat, scorching her problems away.

"No," Alanna said aloud, but her voice sounded weak even to her. "I can't. Conner would hate me. He'd be crushed. I can't do that to him."

*Who cares about Conner? He's not here now. He wasn't there when you called. He obviously doesn't care about you.*

Alanna knew this train of thought was insane. She knew Conner had the right to be wherever he wanted to be on a Friday night. It wasn't like they had plans. But the little voice inside her head made it all sound so easy. Made everything so clear and simple.

Conner didn't care about her. Her parents didn't care about her. Why should *she* care about her? She was obviously worthless. *And worthless people drink. It's all they have.*

Alanna took a deep breath and held it. She glanced at the phone, glanced at the door. The phone. The door. The phone.

And then she was out the door.

# Jessica Wakefield

I was right in the middle of cheering my little butt off for Ken, pretty much high on adrenaline, when I caught a glimpse of Jeremy in the stands and my spirited little heart stopped beating. He's with Trent, and they both look really serious. Now, Jeremy has a tendency to look serious for no apparent reason sometimes, but Trent?

That boy couldn't stop smiling if someone yanked out all his teeth.

When I saw his face, I knew I was in trouble. Jeremy was leaving. I knew that. But the moment I saw them, I knew it was happening sooner than any of us had thought. Maybe tomorrow. Maybe tonight.

After that I just don't feel much like cheering.

# Jeremy Aames

I didn't want Jessica to see me. I knew if she took one look at me, she'd know something was up. But there were no seats left in the back. The seniors at every school pretty much commandeer that area. The only spots Trent and I could squeeze into were right up front next to an elderly couple wearing more SVH paraphernalia than I knew existed up until now.

I saw Jessica see me and I saw the look on her face and it broke my heart. This is a night we are both going to remember for the rest of our lives.

# CHAPTER
## The Bad Guy

"Come on, man!" Josh Radinsky yelled, getting right up in Ken's face. Their masks knocked together, and Ken took a step back but then pushed forward again just to show he was holding his ground. "Keep it together, Matthews! What the hell is wrong with you!?"

"Hey, hey, hey!" Todd shouted, coming up next to them. "Knock it off! We can't fall apart now!" Todd managed to pull Josh away from Ken, but the anger in Josh's eyes had already seared its way into Ken's brain.

He was screwing everything up. Big time.

How could this entire game have turned on him so fast? One second they were scoring the most beautiful touchdown he'd ever thrown, the next second, it seemed, he'd been sacked for a loss and thrown a near interception. If the guy on the Lions' defense hadn't basically tripped himself, Santa Carla would have the ball right now.

"Come on, man, what's the play?" one of Ken's teammates shouted as he approached the huddle.

"Okay, forty-five fake reverse, on two," Ken said, trying to work some confidence back into his tone. "Break!"

"Hut one! Hike!" he shouted from the line. The ball was thrust into his hands and Ken looked up for Tony, but before he could even blink, he saw a huge defender coming at him from the corner of his eye. Ken tried to tuck the ball, but the guy reached out a meaty hand and batted it away. In seeming slow motion Ken felt the ball stripped from his fingers and watched it bounce off the toe of his cleat and into the waiting hands of a Lions defenseman.

He squeezed his eyes shut as the announcer roared, "Matthews's fumble picked up by Gliberman. Lions, first down!"

Ken ripped off his chin guard and jogged over to Coach Riley, knowing the man was salivating to chew him out. Riley, red faced as always, stormed over to him.

"Focus, son!" he shouted, slapping Ken's helmet a few times. "Where's your focus? What do you think you're playing out there, some midseason throwaway game?"

"No, Coach," Ken shouted back since that was what was expected of him. The shouting actually made him feel a bit better. It took away the hollow, disappointed pain in his chest for a split second.

"What are you playing for?" Coach Riley yelled, gripping his face mask.

"The championship, Coach!" Ken yelled so hard, his throat hurt.

"Well, act like it!" Coach shouted. He flung Ken's mask away, whipping his head to the side and throwing him off balance. "Now get the hell out of my face until we get the ball back!"

Ken took a step away and grabbed a plastic water cup, dumping its contents all over his face. *Just don't let them score,* he thought as he glanced up at the board. It was tied, seven-seven. If they didn't score and he could get back out there and do something, all would not be lost.

But on the next play the Lions' quarterback threw a perfect pass to a wide receiver who was just sitting in the end zone like no one had even bothered to cover him. The SVH crowd behind him let out one big, anguished groan that seemed to be directed right at Ken.

Ken's head dropped forward. His heart felt like it had been trampled by the opposing team's cleats. He knew Hank Krubowski was somewhere on this sideline, but he was afraid to even look around. The SVH fans started booing, and Ken let the sound wash over him. It seemed right. He was the bad guy here. In ten seconds he'd probably just smashed their hopes, his dreams, and the rest of his life. If he hadn't coughed up the ball, they'd still be tied.

This was not the kind of play top schools rewarded with scholarships.

Conner swung the Mustang into his driveway on Friday night, killed the lights, and just sat there for a moment. It was a beautiful night. The breeze was blowing, the air smelled sweet, and he just wanted to savor the feeling of being home, being in his car, feeling . . . good. He took a deep breath, ran his hand across the dashboard, and sighed. Then he scoffed at himself.

"Freak," he muttered. He got out of the car and pulled out his guitar case. The reason he was in such a good mood had nothing to do with the beautiful weather. He'd just had one of the better guitar lessons of his life. It was the first really solid one since he'd been back from rehab. Today it had felt like he'd never stopped playing. In fact, he seemed to be playing better than ever. Gavin had told him he was really progressing, and Conner could hear it too. So much for the theory that drunks made better artists.

He walked into the foyer and was about to head

upstairs to play a little while longer when Megan walked in from the family room. She was wearing her glasses, and her hair was pulled back in a ponytail, which made it obvious she'd been studying. Conner was about to give her his standard Megan-is-a-geek ribbing when she cut him off.

"Good, you're home," she said, pushing up the sleeves of her sweater.

"What's wrong?" Conner asked, knowing instantly from her tone that something had upset her. He placed the guitar down against the wall, never taking his eyes off his sister.

"It's just Alanna called a while ago. . . ."

Conner's heart skipped a few sickening beats. "And?" he prompted.

Megan shrugged and looked off to the side. "I don't know, she just sounded kind of upset."

The sickened feeling spread out from his heart to his gut. "Did she say what was wrong?" he asked, clenching his jaw. "Was it her parents?" Conner was surprised by the force of emotion that swept over him. A protective instinct kicked in that he hadn't felt since Elizabeth had pulled a few stupid moves earlier in the year.

"I don't know," Megan repeated, throwing up her hands and letting them slap down at her sides. "All she said was to call her the second you got home."

Conner pulled out his keys and spun around. "I'll be back later," he said, flinging open the door.

"Where're you going?" Megan called after him as he jogged down the front walk.

Conner didn't bother answering. Megan was a smart kid. She could figure it out. He was revving the engine before he even had both feet in the car. As he peeled out into the street, a million things flooded his mind. What if her parents had gone beyond yelling and hurt her? What if one of her ex-boyfriends had dropped by and tried to get her to drink? What if she'd had a drink all on her own?

He threw the car into fourth gear and pounded on the gas. Alanna's place was twenty minutes away when he drove the speed limit. He'd get there in ten.

Will checked his watch and added the exact time the halftime whistle blew to his list of stats. He glanced out at the teams as they headed off to the locker rooms for the halftime break and felt a pang of nostalgia, but he pushed it away when he imagined the verbal beating the team was about to take. The score was fourteen to seven in favor of the Lions, and the Gladiators had looked like peewee players in the second quarter. Riley was going to throw a fit. Will shook his head and smiled. Maybe he was better off in the stands.

He closed his notebook and jogged down the stairs in the center of the stands. Mr. Matthews needed these stats before halftime was over, so he had to get up to the press box. He made his way around to the back of the stands and started to climb the aluminum steps that led to the box, but when he was halfway up, he spotted Mr. Matthews on the path that led to the concession stand. There were hundreds of people milling around, but Will could tell Mr. Matthews was talking to someone. He squinted and focused, and his heart dropped when he realized who Mr. Matthews's companion was. Hank Krubowski.

Right. According to Krubowski's letter, they were supposed to be meeting now. Will had gotten so wrapped up in doing his job, he'd almost forgotten. Now was his one and only chance to find out the truth . . . if he had the guts.

At that moment the mike flicked on with a squeal. "Ladies and gentlemen, please give a warm welcome to your Sweet Valley High varsity cheerleaders!" The halftime-routine music blared from the speakers, and Will looked out onto the field to see Melissa jogging out, grinning with the rest of the girls. There was no way she could have noticed Matthews and Krubowski. He glanced over at the pair again, and they were disappearing around the back of the Snack Shack, as the concession stand was affectionately called. Will hesitated one moment before tearing back down the stairs.

His heart was pounding and his fingers stuck to his pad as he dodged and wove through the crowd on his way to the Shack. There was a huge line at the window, and Will didn't see either of the men anywhere. He walked around the side of the shack, where a couple of middle schoolers were hanging out eating hot dogs, and crept to the corner, holding his breath. He froze when he heard Krubowski's voice, stage whispering to be heard over the noisy crowd.

"So we're all set?" Krubowski asked.

"Yeah, yeah, yeah," Matthews responded. "You're in for the assistant coaching position."

Will's blood roared in his ears. So there *was* some kind of trade-off going on here. *Stay calm,* he told himself. *You don't know anything yet.* But there were two grown men hiding out in the weeds behind the Snack Shack, whispering about—

"You're sure?" Krubowski said. "Because if I have to play the lackey for one more season—"

"Don't worry about it. I told you my connections would come through for you," Mr. Matthews said. "To tell you the truth, I think I got the better end of the bargain. They really liked you at Southern Cal. You're definitely qualified for the job."

"And your boy is qualified for the team," Krubowski said. "Or I thought he was before tonight—no offense."

"None taken," Mr. Matthews said. Will heard a slapping sound and could imagine Mr. Matthews clapping Krubowski on the back. "Just wait until the second half. He just got a little overconfident, but he won't let us down."

"Let's hope not," Krubowski said.

Mr. Matthews snorted a laugh. "C'mon, Coach, I'll treat you to a hot dog."

Will's heart leaped into his throat as he heard the weeds start to rustle and crack. He ducked around the front of the Snack Shack and cut in front of the line so it would look like he'd been waiting there for a while.

"Hey!" the lady behind him protested.

"Andy! Just give me a Coke," Will said, slapping down a dollar. Andy Marsden, who sometimes worked the Shack at halftime, slid a can across the counter.

"Looks like you've got trouble, man," Andy said with a grin, nodding toward the line of angry customers.

"Yeah," Will answered. Andy had no idea how right he was. Will ducked his head and rushed away without even looking at the offended people. He glanced up at Matthews and Krubowski, who were waiting on line as he walked by, but they were so engrossed in conversation, they never even noticed him. Will let out a sigh of relief. He wasn't sure he could act cool right now if he tried.

Over the hundreds of thoughts combating for attention in his head, two things were abundantly clear. He was sitting on the biggest scandal of the year. And he had no idea what to do about it.

# Conner McDermott

Okay, Megan's been known to be a little bit melodramatic at times. So just because her conversation with Alanna got her freaked out doesn't mean anything's really wrong. It could be anything. It doesn't mean it has to do with her evil parents. And it definitely doesn't mean Alanna's about to take a drink or anything.

Man, am I going to hit _every_ red light on the way to this girl's house?

# Will Simmons

What am I going to do? I'm stunned. Completely stunned.

I mean, I suspected something was going on, but hearing it with my own ears is a different thing. It's sickening, actually.

But forget that. What should I do?

I should keep quiet. That's what I should do. If I had never taken the job at the _Tribune,_ I would have no idea this was going on. And I never would have gotten the job at the _Trib_ if it wasn't for Mr. Matthews. I can't turn him in. There's no way. Besides, I'd lose my job. And I love my job. It's the only thing I like in my life right now, actually (besides Melissa, of course).

And when I really think about it, who's going to suffer if I tell what I heard? Ken, right? And yeah, there was a point in time when I would have loved to see that, but now . . . I mean, it's not like _Ken_ has done anything wrong. He's just living his dream. And to be honest, if I gave him up, it would just be from spite. Because he's living _my_ dream too. And yeah, it sucks, but it's not his fault. In a lot of ways it's mine.

The thing is, a lot of people will think it's suspicious if Ken gets a scholarship after the first half he played. But if he does really well in the second half . . . well . . . if he does well, it'll be no big deal. No one will ever know.

As long as I keep my mouth shut.

## No Thanks to Me

"Time-out! Sweet Valley High! This is their last time-out!" The announcer's voice sizzled over the loudspeaker, seeming to fry Ken's nerves as he jogged over to the sideline to find out what Riley's game plan was. He looked up at the scoreboard, knowing exactly what it said—the same thing it had said since early in the third quarter when Micah Grant had successfully kicked an SVH field goal. Home: 10, Visitor: 14. The score wouldn't have been that bad if not for the other figures on the clock. Quarter: 4, Time Remaining: 00:32.

Ken had thirty-two seconds to score a touchdown. To win the game. To salvage his career. To change the rest of his life.

"Okay, Matthews," Riley said, holding out his clipboard, where a play was drawn out with $x$'s and $o$'s. He put his hand on Ken's shoulder as they both bent over the play. "I want you to fake a pass, then hand the ball off to Lucia. He'll run the reverse, and hopefully it'll confuse these guys enough so he can get in for the score."

Ken felt like the wind had been knocked out of him. They were on the fifty-yard line. Everyone knew that the only way they could win was with a touchdown, and the only way they could score a touchdown was if Ken threw the ball. The only reason Riley would call a fake reverse was if he had no faith in Ken—not that he could entirely blame him. Ken had been pretty ineffective in the second half, but at least he hadn't made any major mistakes.

"Coach," Ken began, his heart pounding hard. No one ever second-guessed Riley, but if he didn't say something, he knew he'd always regret it. "Don't you think—"

"I know what you're going to say, Matthews," Riley said gruffly, keeping his voice down. "But you've done a great job of keeping the ball this quarter. Their defense is tired. They won't expect the run, and I'm banking that once they see Lucia tearing down the field, it'll be too late."

Ken sighed but squared his shoulders. "But Coach—"

"Ken!" Riley barked. "Get in there and call this play!" The two men locked eyes, neither one willing to back down. Ken just wanted to shake the guy. They were never going to win this way.

"Let's go, Coach," the ref yelled, indicating that

the time-out was over. Ken blinked, but Riley's face was as hard as stone. Ken wasn't going to win this one. As he jogged out onto the field, his mind was reeling. *We can't run,* he thought. *If we run, we're screwed. We're done. There's no way they're going to let Lucia get into the end zone.*

He joined the rest of the team in the huddle, feeling like he had the weight of the world on his back. Every single thing in his life was riding on this next play—the pride of the school, the respect of his teammates, his potential scholarship, his father's opinion of him. He looked at the scoreboard again and a nervous, anticipatory jolt shot down his spine. Suddenly Ken knew what he had to do.

"Todd . . . Josh," Ken said, glancing at each of them in the huddle. "Just get open." They nodded, and the whole team looked at each other. They knew this was it. One more play and the season was over. "It's do-or-die time," Ken said. "On three. Ready, break!"

*If this doesn't work, I am so dead,* Ken told himself as he lined up for the play. *Dead, dead, dead, dead, dead.* He saw Riley pacing the sideline and told himself to concentrate. It would all be over soon, one way or the other.

"Blue thirteen! Blue thirteen! Hut, hut, hike!" Ken shouted. The ball was in his hands. He dropped back to pass.

"Matthews! What the hell are you *doing!*" Riley shouted from the sideline.

Ken scanned the field, spotted Josh wide open, and let the ball fly. *This is it. This is it! It's perfect!* Ken thought. But then, seemingly out of nowhere, a Santa Carla cornerback came flying across the field and picked the ball out of the air right in front of Josh.

On instinct Ken immediately started rushing across the field to stop the defender, but his mind was no longer on the game. It was like his life was flashing before his eyes. He saw the cornerback break a tackle, spin around, slam into another SVH guy and send him sprawling.

*It's over,* Ken thought. *They're going to score. They're going to win. And it's all my fault.*

Then, as if by some miracle, Todd raced up behind the cornerback and reached around him. The ball was knocked loose as Todd lost his footing and crashed to the ground, bringing the cornerback with him.

"Get the ball!" Ken heard himself shout as he rushed forward. It hit the ground and bounced a few times, and then someone grabbed it. Ken looked up, hoping against hope that it was one of his guys.

"And Radinsky picks up the fumble!"

The crowd went insane. Josh stood up and started to run, looking over his shoulder, but there was no one anywhere near him. One second ago every player on the field had been busy running in the other direction, and now he had an open field.

"He's at the fifty! The forty! The thirty! No one's even close! The ten! The five! Score!" The buzzer pealed, indicating the end of the fourth quarter. "SVH wins! SVH wins!" the announcer shouted. "What a play!"

The noise was practically deafening as Ken tore down the field with the rest of his teammates and piled on top of Josh. The sounds of a million cheering voices filled his ears as Todd hugged him.

"We won! We won!" Todd yelled.

Ken smiled and put on a good show, trying to join in the elation of his teammates, but he couldn't quite muster up the joy. Yes, they'd won. But it was no thanks to him.

Jessica didn't even know who she was hugging as she jumped up and down, screaming her lungs out on the sidelines, but she also didn't care. She'd never seen anything like the play that had just transpired on the field. She was going to have to give Josh Radinsky a big, fat kiss for that one—she didn't care how much of a jerk he was.

As the team ran off the field, helmets held aloft in victory, Jessica and the rest of the cheerleaders tore out to meet them, and soon the stands were emptying too. The announcer was shouting something about an SVH record for fumble return, and Tia was screaming so loud in Jessica's ear, she thought her eardrum was going to pop out. Jessica felt like she was running on air. There was nothing in the world like a good adrenaline rush.

"Ken! Ken!" Jessica and Tia yelled, running over to him. They hugged him, and he twirled them both around.

"Good game!" Jessica shouted, grinning. "Congratulations."

"Yeah, right," Ken scoffed, keeping up his smile at the same time. He ran his hand over his sweaty blond hair. "I had nothing to do with it."

"Please!" Tia said, slapping his shoulder pad as the rest of the school partied all around them. "If you hadn't scored that first-quarter touchdown, we wouldn't have won, right?"

"I guess you have a point," Ken said sheepishly. He glanced over their shoulders and lifted his chin. "Hey, thanks, guys. I'm gonna go get Maria."

He jogged off, and Tia joined a group of SVH athletes who were all trying to lift Josh onto their shoulders. Jessica laughed as she watched them struggle with his not so heavy weight just because too many people were trying to lift him at once. Right as she was about to join the craziness, she felt someone grab her from behind around her waist.

Jessica spun around and looked right into Jeremy's

deep brown eyes. "Hi!" she shouted to be heard over the mayhem. A tight vise seemed to squeeze her chest as the memory flooded back of what he was there to tell her. But she had to try to let this moment last a little longer before his words punctured the excitement. She threw her arms around Jeremy and hugged him. "Wasn't that a great game?"

"Yeah, congratulations!" Jeremy yelled, replacing her on the ground. "I've never seen anything like that last play. Who is that guy?"

Jessica laughed and looked over her shoulder at Josh, who was finally up and being carried around on the team's shoulders. He had his helmet in one hand and the game ball in the other and was cheering like a madman.

"That's Josh Radinsky," Jessica said, looking back up at Jeremy. "Or as he will probably be known from now on, 'the boy with the biggest ego in town.'"

"Yeah, well, he deserves it," Jeremy said. He smiled down at her, and his face suddenly turned serious. With a massive heart flop Jessica realized she couldn't avoid this any longer. It was time to face Jeremy's bad news, and there was no more hiding behind chatting about SVH's big win as if it was the only thing going on tonight. Suddenly all the raucous, joyous noise around her faded into an irritating buzz.

"So, what's up?" Jessica asked. "I, um, I didn't

know you were coming to the game tonight."

"I was just thinking . . . ," Jeremy said, picking up her right hand with his left and lacing his fingers through hers, then doing the same with his other hand. "You should enjoy this victory while it lasts."

*Because you're leaving,* Jessica thought, staring at the ground. *Because in a few minutes I'm going to be devastated.*

"Why do you say that?" she asked, tears filling her eyes, causing the matted grass beneath her feet to blur.

"Because with me as captain, Big Mesa is going to kick your sorry Sweet Valley butts in basketball this year," Jeremy said.

Jessica's head snapped up, and for a second she just stared at Jeremy's grinning face, totally certain she hadn't heard him right. With him as captain? Did he really mean . . . ? A pleasant tingle zipped over her entire body.

"You're staying?" Jessica demanded, searching his sparkling eyes. "You're staying?"

"I'm staying," Jeremy said, squeezing her hands.

Jessica threw herself into his arms so hard, he had to take a couple of steps back to keep his balance, but once he caught himself, he spun her around and around until the whole field was one big streak of color. Jessica felt like she was going to keep spinning giddily forever even after he put her down.

"Guys! Guys!" Andy came running up to them through the crowd, Elizabeth, Tia, and Trent in tow. "C'mon! We're going out to celebrate! Are you coming?"

"Are you kidding?" Jessica asked, clutching Jeremy's hand after he released her. "We wouldn't miss it." Especially now that they *really* had something to celebrate.

Jessica looked up at Jeremy, and he leaned down and kissed her—a long, sweet kiss—and Jessica couldn't have been happier to know that it was the first of many more to come.

"Hey! There's the championship QB!" Maria called out gleefully, running up to Ken on the sidelines with a mini pom-pom sticking out of the pocket of her jacket. The moment Ken saw her, he realized he actually would rather not talk to her right now. He was so depressed about his performance, he didn't even want to see Maria. *That* was pretty bad.

"Hey," he said when she threw her arms around him. He tried to release her quickly, but Maria hung on.

"I'm so proud of you, Ken," she whispered in his ear, giving him a kiss on the cheek. Proud? Ken couldn't imagine why. Had she seen the same game the rest of the crowd had? None of them had missed how much he'd sucked. People were coming up to him and politely congratulating him, but he could tell by their tight smiles that they knew exactly what he knew—they probably would have all been better off with Will Simmons out there on the field. It was pretty crazy that Maria was finally excited about how he played on the field—after being against his taking over the star-quarterback role for so long—and he hadn't even done anything for her to be excited about.

"What's wrong?" Maria asked, taking a step back and studying his face.

"Nothing," Ken said. "Can we just get out of here? I want to get home."

Maria's face scrunched up in concern. "Wait, don't you have to meet with Krubowski?" she asked, walking quickly to catch up with him since he'd already taken off in the direction of the school. "And everyone's going out to celebrate."

"I'm not really in the mood," Ken said, rubbing his itchy, sweaty forehead with his fingertips. He was exhausted but tense at the same time. He just wanted to get changed and get the heck out of there before Krubowski tracked him down to tell him the scholarship was going to someone else.

"Ken?"

Ken's heart fell. Oh, well. Too late. He turned around to face Hank Krubowski and his fate.

"Hi, Mr. Krubowski," Ken said, feeling like he could cry right there. Instead he tried to steel himself for the worst. He just hoped the guy made it quick and painless.

"Congratulations, son," Krubowski said, thrusting out his hand. Ken just stared at it. "The scholarship is yours."

Ken looked up at Maria, trying to process what he'd just heard, and she was grinning from ear to ear.

"Well, shake the man's hand!" she said, nudging his shoulder.

Ken smiled and clasped Krubowski's hand, shocked at the power behind his own grip. He'd thought he didn't have an ounce of strength left in him, but suddenly he felt like he could take on the whole Santa Carla team himself.

"Don't look so surprised," Krubowski said, clapping Ken on the shoulder with his free hand. "You showed real determination in the face of Jake Barrow, and you controlled the ball like a pro in the second half. You kept your cool, and that's just as important a quality in a quarterback as a good arm. There are going to be games where you're not at your best, but as long as you can hold your own and pull through it with a win like this, you're doing okay."

"Thank you!" Ken said, laughing. He couldn't believe the force of the elation that was rushing through him. "Thank you so much!"

Krubowski smiled kindly. "Michigan will be proud to have you, son," he said. Then he stuffed his hands in his pockets and smirked. "Just work those interceptions, would ya?" he joked.

"I will!" Ken said good-naturedly. Krubowski nodded and walked off, and Ken completely lost it. He yelled with joy and picked Maria up off the ground, sitting her butt on his forearms and twirling her around. "I'm going to Michigan! I'm going to Michigan!"

"I got it!" Maria shouted, laughing as she pounded on his shoulders. "Put me down already!"

He released her, and Maria pulled him to her for a nice, long victory kiss. Ken had never felt so relieved and happy in his life. SVH had won the state championship, and the only dream he'd had since he was a little kid was about to come true. He was going to play college ball at the University of Michigan.

Maria broke away, and they stood there just grinning at each other, soaking up the cheers, the sound of the band, and the joy all around them. For that one moment all was right in Ken's world.

*Everything's going to be fine,* Conner told himself, feeling uncharacteristically jittery as he walked up the steps to Alanna's front door. He was sure she'd just gotten into a minor argument with her parents or something. She'd probably been really upset when she called Megan because it had just happened, and by now he was certain she had calmed herself down and was feeling much better.

He just hoped she hadn't calmed herself down by taking a drink.

A cool breeze skittered past him as he reached out to ring the doorbell, and it sent a foreboding chill down his spine.

"Don't jump to conclusions," he whispered under his breath. He knew he wouldn't appreciate it if everyone just assumed *he* was going to get drunk every time something went wrong.

The door swung open slowly, and there Alanna stood, clad in a pair of gray sweats and a black, battered SVU sweatshirt. Her face was puffy as if she'd been crying, and her eyes were all watery, but she looked like the worst was over.

"Hi," she said tentatively. "You didn't have to come over."

"Are you okay?" Conner asked, wanting to reach out and touch her but somehow feeling like he shouldn't.

Alanna sniffled and managed a smile. "I am now," she said, practically falling into his arms.

Conner hugged her there in the open doorway, wondering what to say. He'd never been good at this kind of thing, but he wanted to be there for Alanna if he could. He cared about her so much, it almost hurt.

"Let's go in," Conner said finally. Alanna released him and backed away, holding the door open for him as he stepped inside. "So what happened?" he asked, stuffing his hands into the front pockets of his jeans.

"My parents," Alanna said with a rueful laugh. She shook her head, causing her curls to fall all around her shoulders. "You'd think I'd be used to them by now." Hugging herself, Alanna looked everywhere but at his face. Her gaze flicked from the hardwood floor to the umbrella stand to the doorway into the next room, but never at his face.

"I don't think you ever get used to parents," Conner said, hoping to get her to look at him. She didn't, so Conner reached up and tugged at her sleeve. "Come on. We'll go put on some bad Friday-night movie."

Alanna smiled, and it made Conner's heart go warm. " 'Kay," she said, leading the way into the TV room. On the way there Conner happened to glance into her father's study, and what he saw there made his blood run cold. The liquor cabinet was wide open, and there was a bottle of scotch on the desk with a half-empty glass next to it, leaving a sweat ring on the leather desk pad.

"Alanna?" Conner said, his voice laced with tension.

She came back and glanced into the room. "Oh, my dad always has a drink before he goes out," she said, waving her hand. She reached around him to pull the door closed, and Conner could have sworn he smelled scotch on her breath. The tangy, sweet scent made his stomach clench.

*You're just imagining it,* he told himself. *The smell is probably just coming from the room.*

She smiled up at him and continued on her way to the TV room. Conner followed slowly, wanting to believe her—wanting to believe his own little inner voice—but he couldn't make himself relax. He had a bad feeling about this.

In the TV room Alanna gestured at the couch for Conner to sit down, and he did, trying to watch her without looking like he was watching her. She wasn't acting strangely. She definitely didn't *seem* drunk. As she lay down on the couch and put her head in his lap, he used his fingertips to gently brush a few tendrils of hair off her face.

"I'm glad you're here," Alanna said, sounding like a little girl.

"Me too," Conner said sincerely. As he sat there looking down at her face, he knew it didn't matter whether or not she'd had a drink tonight. He cared about her, and he was already in too deep.

There was no going back now.

# ALANNA FELDMAN

## 12:05 A.M.

Conner just left, and I cleaned up my dad's study. I hope it looks okay in there. The sweat ring was a pain to deal with, but it's probably fine now. I don't think anyone will know the difference.

But did Conner know? I mean, the second I saw his car pull up, I downed like half a bottle of mouthwash, so maybe I'm okay. I just couldn't tell. I think he believed my story, but he's not stupid. He's been there. He knows.

All I'm sure of is I can't lose Conner. I can't. I really don't know what will happen to me if I do.

# CONNER MCDERMOTT

## 12:05 A.M.

She was drinking. I know she was. I could tell by the way she was acting. She kept bringing it up all night. Saying stuff like, "I don't know why my father drinks scotch. I can't stand the taste of it," and, "I hate my dad's study. Isn't it gross? So stuffy. I never even go in there." She was obviously trying to cover.

I'm such an idiot. What am I supposed to do? I should dump her. I know I should. I can't have a person like that in my life right now. Not after everything I've learned.

But what kind of person am I if I don't help her?

# JESSICA WAKEFIELD
## 12:07 A.M.

Jeremy just dropped me off. We left the last victory party around eleven and went to Crescent Beach, just the two of us, to, you know, celebrate the fact that he's not moving. Let's just say there was <u>lots</u> of kissing going on. Ahhh. He's such a good kisser.

He told me his parents left the final decision up to him, and you know what? That just makes the fact that he's staying so much sweeter. He chose California. He chose me. He's always asking me what he has to do to prove to me that he cares about me. Well, that pretty much sealed the deal. I know it now for sure.

He really does love me.

# TIA RAMIREZ

## 12:08 A.M.

HMMM . . . WAS IT ME, OR WAS TRENT FLIRTING WITH ME TONIGHT? I HAD TO BE IMAGINING IT. RIGHT?

I MEAN, ALL THAT STUFF HAS BEEN OVER BETWEEN US FOR A LONG TIME NOW. OF COURSE, THAT WAS BACK WHEN I WAS STILL WITH ANGEL, AND NOW I'M AS SINGLE AS I COULD POSSIBLY BE. . . .

I'LL GET ANDY'S OPINION TOMORROW.

# KEN MATTHEWS

## 12:08 A.M.

I can't believe I'm home right now. I could party for another five hours at least. I'm so pumped! Aaaaaahhh! I can't believe I'm going to Michigan! I had the best time tonight. It was like no one remembered my crappy performance, or at least they didn't care. For once the whole team was together with no ego crap, nothing. We just went crazy and had an amazing time, and I'm going to remember it for the rest of my life.

Everything came together tonight. And nothing's ever going to bring me down.

# WILL SIMMONS
## 12:18 A.M.

I can't sleep. I just hope I'm doing the right thing. I know I am. Ken deserves everything he's gotten. It's not his fault I got hurt. I can't take my crap out on him. I know what his dad and Krubowski are doing isn't right, but what's the point of turning them in? They'd be punished, but so would Ken. And there's no real reason for that. So I'm just going to keep my mouth shut, and everything will work out. Ken keeps his scholarship to Michigan, and I keep my job at the Trib.

# MELISSA FOX

## 12:19 A.M.

First thing tomorrow I am calling Will to get the real deal on Ken's scholarship. And if Will was right and Hank Krubowski was bribed, then Ken's going to know. I don't care what Will says—something that big can't stay a secret.